THE SIGNALMAN'S SHED

The Blum Gatley Stories

BARRY WOODWARD

Lydiate Series One

A black and white photograph

It's a class photo taken in my first year at the church primary school.

My face is fresh, my eyes bright and innocent. It's like seeing a ghost.

Another boy tries to avoid the camera lens, declines to smile and averts his eyes. He twists to one side, his gangling arms wrapped around the back of his seat. It seems an effort to confine himself to his place in class.

It's obvious he doesn't want to be there.

He is Blum Gatley – a practical joker and a thief, with a talent for revenge.

But he wasn't all bad.

We met on our first day at school and he was my friend all his life.

The times we spent together made me feel alive...

CONTENTS

The Signalman's Shed

THE LONG BLACK shed that dominated the Signalman's ramshackle cottage garden had always intrigued Blum and me. It had no windows and nobody we knew had ever seen inside. He didn't keep hens and his work in the garden didn't go beyond planting a few vegetables. Yet it was the biggest garden shed we'd ever known and we saw no purpose for the tarred and felted monolith. It was a mystery we wanted to solve.

In those days, before the private housing estates invaded the parish, you could approach the cottage across the fields, but between his garden and the closest field lay a deep ditch backed by a hedge of hawthorn, holly and hazel that had not been cut in years.

Three times, we'd attempted to cross the ditch for a sneak around. On two occasions -- I don't know how -- the Signalman had detected our trespass within minutes, appeared at a gap in the hedge, shouted at us to clear off; and on the second, fired a shotgun over our heads.

This was the wrong reaction from the property owner, for it made Blum even more interested in what the Signalman had to hide. In fact, it became a minor obsession. Why was he so protective of his unkempt garden and house? Was it something to do with his shed?

The third time, one Mischief Night, we took battery torches and streaked our faces with mud like commandoes to cross the ditch, to see what we could discover about the Signalman's shed. It was a failed mission.

We jumped the ditch, pushed into the hedge and stumbled into a trip wire, which set off a cacophony of rattling cans and buckets, then a loud bang. Blum was convinced it was some ancient spring gun device to kill trespassers. I thought it more likely the Signalman had again took up his shotgun. Anyway, we escaped intact, ran for our lives across a twenty-acre spud field. I never wanted to go near the place again.

I was startled one day the following summer when Blum called at our house and announced in an urgent, hushed voice that today we would raid the Signalman's shed.

'No! Not a chance!' I said. 'He's mad. If he catches us, he'll kill us!'

Blum grabbed my shoulder, his face full of excitement. 'He's blummin' dead! Three weeks since. I've only just found out!'

Blum's mam had heard the news that morning, having missed market day for near a month owing to a bout of shingles. The Signalman had paid for his order at the Co-Op and dropped dead. He was cremated at a cheerless ceremony where the only mourner present was an official from British Railways, which had taken into nationalisation the old railway company for whom the Signalman worked for forty-odd years.

Everybody called him the Signalman, but the dead man had not pulled any levers in the old signal box on the moss for a long time. He was pensioned off when the branch line was closed soon after the war. While the sleepers and rails were torn up for salvage, he was allowed to live out his retirement at Signalman's cottage. Ever the company man, he continued to wear his railway uniform; shiny-peaked, flat hat, grey serge trousers, matching jacket with railway insignia and a waistcoat with silver watch and chain. He wore it on his final visit to the Co-Op.

In recent times he was rarely seen out and about. He was always a bit of a loner, the locals said. I could remember as a kid him strutting past my grandmother's shop. My dad once commented, 'Eh, up, there's Adolf, *der* Signalman. *Achtung*! *Achtung*!' It was some time before I realised he was comparing the Signalman to Hitler. I saw why. He still had black hair even at his age. A fringe pushed to one side gave him the look of *Der Fuehrer,* compounded by a paintbrush moustache.

I'd seen pictures of Hitler in a slide show at school, as well as images of the Nazi SS in their uniforms and their defiant, cruel faces at the Nuremburg Trials. What they'd done in the war haunted my dreams for a long time. Even dad's name for him -- *Der* Signalman -- became sinister, like the ranks of *Gruppenfuehrer, Hauptsturmfuehrer* and *Der Fuehrer* himself, synonymous with the photographs I'd seen in a book of his; blurred images of death camps and railway trucks packed with doomed Jews.

I was reluctant, but Blum was insistent we went straight to the Signalman's cottage. He was anxious that railway workmen would invade and destroy the whole place before he could satisfy his curiosity. This was possible as not long before two disused track workers' cottages had fallen into such disrepair they were demolished.

When we walked down the straight black clinker track, sleepers, rails and ballast, long gone, it was clear a demolition crew had not visited. Larks sang in a blue sky. The tall hedges moved in the breeze and the Signalman's cottage looked the same as ever, except for the lack of smoke from the chimney.

Blum talked non-stop. He speculated on what we'd find. His favourite theory was that the Signalman had stolen a steam loco, dismantled it and hidden it away for his own private pleasure. But it could be treasure. Would it be sacks of gold sovereigns, or diamonds and rubies? Or even a consignment of bombs and guns stolen during the War? Why was the Signalman so keen to keep people away from his home? Even Big John from the Co-Op, we'd heard, was discouraged from knocking and left the monthly groceries order in a rabbit hutch arrangement by the Signalman's front door. Visitors were not encouraged. There had to be a reason.

My mind was so full of wild fears I let Blum talk without comment. I forced myself not to imagine the Signalman was some mad Nazi who had undertaken horrible experiments with people he'd kidnapped along the disused railway tracks before hiding the unspeakable evidence in the sinister black shed. I was nervous as we reached our destination.

When Blum opened the low gate into the small and overgrown front garden, I thought he'd head straight round the back to the shed. Instead he moved to the front door and hammered on it.

'Just making sure,' he said, 'Wouldn't want anyone beatin' us to it, like.'

No answer came to his enthusiastic knocks, so he led the way around the side of the cottage. My heart rate was high and I was ready to leg it at a second's notice, as we approached the back yard and beyond that, the rear door to the house. Inside the flagged yard the green door to an outhouse was ajar.

Blum approached the door. 'Hello?' he called, but again there was no answer.

He pushed the door with his wellie-booted foot, went inside, eyes everywhere. I followed heart in mouth, while he moved around, touching woodwork tools, tins of nails, used paint pots and pieces of off-cut wood.

My eyes were drawn to the floor. Around a copper boiler and the brick fireplace beneath it were stacked bundles of dry twigs. My baseball boots crunched on a layer of dried holly leaves. Then came the smell. It was a pungent, sickly odour, coming from the copper. I stepped forward, peered inside. The bottom of the boiler was covered with a layer of what looked like toffee. The 'toffee,' however, was green. I leaned in, sniffed. The smell was rank.

I turned to Blum, 'What do you reckon this --?'

But Blum cut in, excited, 'Look at these.'

In one hand he held a box of Eley Fourten shotgun cartridges, in the other he flourished a slim red-brown cartridge with a brass base and rim, 'There's two boxes, both near full!'

He jammed the cartridge back in the box. 'I'm going in the house.'

'We can't!'

'No-one's here.'

'It's breaking and entering, burglary! What if ...?'

But Blum was already out of the door. I hurried after him as he went to the back door of the cottage, stopped to peer into the scullery through the dusty window.

'I thought we only came to see in the shed?'

Blum dumped the boxes of cartridges on the window ledge.

'He's got a gun. If these are still here, the gun must be an 'all. It'll be in the house.'

'You can't just go in and take his --

'I only want a couple of shots.'

Blum was mad about guns, any device that fired a missile. He owned and loved catapults, bows and arrows, an air pistol and rifle, even an African spear once owned by his great-grandfather, brought back from the South African wars. Any greedy, bullying starling that raided his mam's bird tables did so at their own risk if Blum was about with his Webley air pistol or B.S.A. air rifle. One day, guns would lead him into trouble.

When he took hold of the door knob, I knew there was nothing I could say that would stop him going inside. Since his father's sudden death, Blum had become more wilful, more reckless, as though he was working through his grief with random actions. Secretly, I hoped the door was locked and bolted, but it creaked open, scraping across the threshold.

'Come on then,' he said, on the brink of burglary, his voice impatient.

I had an instant vision of the pair of us, wearing blazers and school ties, our hair slicked with Brylcream, standing in the dock of an oak-panelled court while a Judge committed us to a reform school and our shamed mothers wept in the public gallery.

'I'll keep watch,' was my lame reply.

Blum was scornful, 'Don't be daft. He's not going to be lying dead in here, is he?'His knowing comment evoked that other time, that other place, when we were younger.

'I know that!' I said, but his jibe hit the bull's-eye. I still remembered in complete detail my only experience of seeing a dead man and my imagination didn't rule out the discovery of another, or even more than a single corpse, especially if we investigated the signalman's shed.

'He's dead and burnt, just ashes, and there's nobody here. Mam said he's no family anyone knows about. Who's going to see us? There's nobody for miles.'

I threw in a last attempt to make him reconsider his entry. 'Harry Catlow passed us on his tractor in Pygon Lane, remember? '

'On his way back from the Plough Horse, ha! He's so drunk he can't remember what happened five minutes ago.'

Which was probably true, so feeling braver, I made a move. Blum entered the scullery and I followed. Though I disliked the Signalman, it still seemed a violation to go into his house without permission. Like most kids I'd been brought up to respect other people's belongings. Or, at least I'd tried. I stepped into the scullery making a mental note not to touch anything, as none of it belonged to me. As long as I kept to that simple code, I wasn't really doing anything wrong, was I? Nor had we broken a window to get inside. The door wasn't even locked, was it?

Blum jostled me aside as he pushed the door closed, looked behind it. I knew what he was doing. Most people who had a gun in those days kept it propped behind the back door, usually loaded, ready to deal with a marauding rat or pigeons and rabbits in the vegetable patch.

'Not there,' he said to himself and turned to scan the mantel shelf over the black, iron oven range and other good places to keep a gun handy. He went to a broom cupboard, rooted through it as I scanned the signalman's scullery.

Everything was neat and clean. For some reason I expected squalor, but there were no dirty pots, or unwashed clothes, no newspapers piled on the table.

A clean white tea towel hung from a nail by the sandstone sink, polished plates filled a beech wood rack. The air in the room was still and warm and though its occupant had been gone for weeks, the odour of fried food, onions, was still present. I began to relax about our trespass.

'Bet yer it's under the stairs,' Blum said.

I looked as he went through the inner door into the hallway. He pulled open the small door under the staircase, dropped to his knees. He scrabbled round, half in, half out of the cupboard, muttering to himself, as he searched. I squeezed past him. Another door, which opened into the parlour, was ajar six inches.

I put my face to the gap and looked through. A shelf clock still ticked away the seconds after its owner's death. I could smell the mustiness of an old man's house, the reek of stale tobacco smoke. A worn leather armchair and a sofa to match both had linen antimacassars and the one on the armchair bore a greasy stain at head height. As the chair was positioned under a standard lamp, alongside a Pye radio set on a small table, I presumed it was the Signalman's usual seat.

I pushed the door open to reveal a sideboard against the back wall. It was huge and ornate. A fancy, engraved mirror stretched up from the body of the sideboard and against it were small, carved shelves to display ornaments. Instead of ornaments, the shelves carried small silver cups like tiny football trophies. Stuck to the mirror were a dozen, or more cards and several rosettes of coloured ribbons.

Curious, without touching, I took a closer look. The cups were engraved with the words British Cage Bird Society. The cards and rosettes had the same words. They were prizes -- prizes for a bird show. So the Signalman was a keeper of birds? Or used to be? One rosette referred to 1927 and a cup for Best in Show was engraved March 1934. I moved to the Signalman's chair. Beside the radio set were a red Oxo stock cube tin and a small, cloth-bound book. I was too curious to resist. I picked up the tin, opened it. Inside was a bundle of ten shilling notes, beneath them a slim wad of postal orders. As soon as I saw money, I clapped the tin shut and replaced it. I didn't even want to experience temptation, let alone give in to it. Yet before I knew what I was doing my hand went to the book.

'I can't find it. Is it in here?' Blum stood in the doorway, scratching at his head.

I looked at him, feeling guilty, putting myself between his eyes and the Oxo tin, failing to take in his question, still troubled by finding money, breaking my determination not to touch someone else's property.

'Sorry, what?'

He was exasperated, 'The blummin' gun!'

His eyes raked all corners of the room then fixed on the sideboard. He stepped forward with a look of anticipation and pulled the lower doors of the sideboard open. He peered inside.

'Jam!' he said, disgusted.

'Eh?

'Stuffed full of the blummin' stuff,' Blum turned away, jabbed his thumb backwards to the sideboard. He put both hands to his head, fingers drumming on his skull.

Then pointed at me, 'Where would you keep a gun if you lived here?'

All I wanted to do was look inside the book, which looked too much like a private diary to resist.

Without thinking, I answered. 'It's probably under the bed.'

Blum was delighted. 'He, he. No wonder he passed the Eleven Plus, eh?'

He vanished in a second, his wellington boots thumped on the wooden staircase, as I turned to the book.

I don't know what I expected to see, but it wasn't a record of victims kidnapped on the deserted railway line. It was a handwritten account book in red ink. Sales of various 'jars' at ten shillings each were recorded in columns alongside names and addresses. The addresses were from all over England and Wales, the names of villages and towns of which I'd never heard. I closed the book and put it aside, thinking about jars. Jars of jam? I moved to the sideboard, stooped down to look inside. The lower cupboards were, indeed, stuffed with jars, dozens of them, but it wasn't jam. I took out a jar, saw its greenish sheen. Was it the same malodorous substance I found in the outhouse copper? Blum's boots sounded on the stairs.

'Nowt out of ten, Brainbox,' he announced at the door, 'Where the blummin' eck would he keep it?'

'Have you looked everywhere?'

'Course I have!' Blum struggled for inspiration. Again, his fingers drummed his head.

'Maybe someone's come and taken it. I mean, he's dead, isn't he? Someone must've been here to… I don't know…'

Blum ignored me then, 'The shed. It'll be in the shed, it's got to be! Leave that blummin' jam!'

'It's not jam,' I said, putting down the jar on the sideboard, but Blum was out of the door. 'Since when's jam been green?' I shouted, hurrying after him, unwilling to be alone in the house.

'My mam does greengage jam, that's green enough,' Blum said as I followed him out of the scullery into the yard. 'Or it might be green tomato chutney.'

'It's the same as the stuff in the outhouse and it stinks.'

Blum strode down the herringbone patterned pathway of old bricks between untended blackcurrant bushes, ragged patches of bolted radish, lettuce and rhubarb.

He approached the shed, which was locked with a hasp and padlock. Without a beat of hesitation he snatched up a garden fork propped against the shed wall and attacked the hasp.

'Don't! You can't do that!'

Walking into an unlocked house was one thing, but this was breaking and entering, vandalism, as well. I was horrified, but it was too late. The pressure of the fork splintered the wood, tore the covering tarred felt. The hasp fell away. Blum jabbed the fork into the earth, pushed in the sagging door. The gloom inside contrasted with outside's sunshine. Blum stepped inside as I peered over his shoulder.

'Got it!' he said with satisfaction. With outstretched hands he reached up. He reminded me of a vicar holding up the communion chalice as he detached a little double-barrelled shotgun from two wooden brackets hanging from a roof truss. The oiled barrels glinted in the sunlight, the varnished walnut stock glowed. Blum pressed his thumb on the lever alongside the lock plate and hammers and the gun snicked open.

'Double barrel,' he said, holding the gun, entranced, like it was some beautiful, live creature.

He squinted up the twin tubes, turning them to the sunlight, 'Lovely and clean.'

He pressed a button and hinged the butt under the barrel to reduce its length to about two feet.

'It's a folding job an' all,' he said, 'A proper poacher's gun.'

I was half listening as I stepped inside the shed. As my eyes adjusted to the dark of the windowless interior, rows of white-painted square objects became visible. I moved a step further, pushing the door wide open. Sunlight streamed in. At once, came the twitter and cheeping of birds, some weak, some stronger.

Blum put the shotgun aside. 'What's this?

I moved down the shed. Small, white square cages with barred fronts were three high along each side of the full length of the shed's interior. I peered into them, and then rushed from one to another. Cage after cage contained a bird, or two, or more, and many of them were dead. In more than one cage were pathetic piles of lifeless birds. Blum was behind me, checking the cages on the opposite side.

My voice cracked, 'There's dozens of them.'

I can't describe how upset I was. The Signalman had died and here in his shed, unknown to anyone, a host of little birds had perished. Others were starving to death, condemned to a terrible end in this locked, unlit monstrosity of a place.

A piercing, repetitive note rose up above the rest of the bird noise.

'It's a yellowhammer!' Blum shouted. He scanned the room, tore open a cage. As reverently as he'd picked up the shotgun, he picked up the bird. Its yellow head and breast appeared to glow in the sunlight. As he held it on his palm, it stood, summoned remaining energy, continued its *chiz-iz-iz-iz-is-zee* like a song of hope.

'Look for the live ones, we've got to blummin' get them out,' Blum said.

He cradled the yellowhammer with his left arm, started to search the cages. I joined him as we checked each cage looked for any sign of life. I recognised linnets and chaffinches. We had the same in our garden at home, but Blum knew them all. He listed them as we gathered up the survivors of this prison. Bullfinches, siskins, redpolls, goldfinches, even a twite, were rescued from their cells.

In ten minutes of frantic to-ing and fro-ing we gathered almost forty birds on a patch of clover surrounded with lovage and tattered foxgloves. Blum examined each one with great care. I did as instructed and fetched mixed seed from a sack in the shed. Some of the weakened birds had already started to eat and the yellowhammer perched in the head of an angelica stalk, sang in the sunshine to celebrate its freedom.

I hurried to fetch a shallow container of water from the house. I marvelled at Blum's gentleness. I'd seen him shoot many a starling in his mother's garden and he was a reformed robber of birds' eggs who would mend a blackbird's broken wing. But I'd also seen him break a rabbit's neck and beat to death with a stick a mother rat and her young. Once, he shot a stoat with a catapult and stamped on its head - - all because he spotted it stalking a thrush. To him, birds were important, but he was never sentimental about them. He shot and poached game birds and wildfowl ate them all his life.

When I got back with the water, Blum's face was red with anger.

'Look at this,' he shouted. 'The cruel, bloody bastard!'

In his hand was a blackthorn twig. Suspended from it by their feet were the shrivelled remains of two goldfinches.

'Bird lime,' he said, with disgust, 'That's how he caught them. That's what that stuff in the copper is, in them blummin' jars. They make it with holly bark. When the bird lands on it, its feet stick -- I bet he was selling it.'

The book and the money now made sense. 'There was a list of addresses in a book.'

Blum ushered me to one side. 'The soddin' bastard was using these and all.'

He steered me behind the clump of angelica, pointed at a square object made of plywood and chicken netting. Inside were the dry corpses of three finches, unidentifiable to me.

'That thing's a call bird trap. Put a hen bird in the middle and its mates will come and get trapped.' he said. 'He'd be selling them to bird keepers for fifteen bob a time.' He paused and spat on the ground. 'I hope the bloody, soddin' bastard rots in hell.'

We spent most of the evening watching and waiting for the birds to recover. Most ate, drank a little water and fluttered away. Some were just too weak to survive. Blum twisted the necks of at least a dozen, buried them beside the clover patch. As he patted down the soil on top of the birds, I could tell he was brooding. When the sun started to sink towards the barley fields, he went to the shed, picked up the shotgun. He broke open the gun and tucked it under his arm.

'What are you doing?' I said. I felt uneasy.

'You don't have to come.'

He strode towards the house. I looked at the remaining birds, still pecking at the pile of seed. My earlier nervousness had returned. I was afraid of what he might do, but couldn't even imagine what that might be, not in the absence of that cruel Signalman, who was the focus of Blum's anger. I remained cross-legged on the clover patch, telling myself to be sensible. There was nothing he could do; about anything. Any idea of revenge was too late.

A few minutes later I heard a shot. An instant later, there was another. The reports sounded flat, unlike a gun. I jumped up, ran to the house. I dashed into the yard, hurdled over a metal drum which now stood by the back door and ran into the scullery.

'Blum!' I shouted.

Two rapid shots exploded. My ears rang as I followed the sound into the parlour. Blum closed the barrels on two more cartridges. He raised the gun, thumbed back the hammers, and shot the sideboard. The mirror smashed and the cups, rosettes and prize cards were blasted all over the room. He fired again, blowing a hole in the back board. I stood open mouthed as he reloaded and reloaded and fired shot after shot into the jars of bird lime, the radio set, the clock, the Oxo tin and finally the back of the armchair right on the greasy patch where the Signalman had rested his head while servicing the orders of other cruel bird keepers, recording his shameful earnings in the account book with its blood-red ink.

When he'd finished he thrust the gun into my hands. Did he expect me to repeat this wanton damage? But he was already on his way out.

'Where're you going?'

He paused at the door. 'This is between me and him that lived here,' he said, 'It's nowt to do with you.'

I stood by, the shotgun in my hands, as Blum splashed the drum of paraffin oil throughout the house. He carried the remaining oil to the black shed.

I followed as Blum made sure all the living birds were now clear and there were none left inside the black shed .He nodded to the gun, 'Put that outside with the rest of the cartridges and meet me at Mullineux's bridge,' he said. 'I won't be long.'

'You can't do this.'

He turned to me. His face was impassive, his voice flat.

'I haven't seen you today. You've never been here.' He stared at me until I understood, nodded agreement, and then he turned away. I watched for perhaps half a minute as he drenched the interior of the black shed with and up-ended the drum in the middle of the floor. Then I left.

Half an hour or so later in the twilight we stood at the top of the hump-back bridge over the cut. Blum now had the folded gun he'd stolen nestled beneath his shirt. His pockets were stuffed with Eley Fourten cartridges.

Out across the moss tall flames from the Signalman's cottage and the black shed pushed showers of orange sparks up into the summer night sky. I felt a sudden, soaring sense of power and exhilaration. I turned to look at Blum's impassive face, then back to the distant inferno.

I was glad *Der* Signalman was dead. I was jubilant at least some of his prisoners had survived and I would never forget the images of death as we liberated the lucky few from that terrible place. But most of all that was when I realised Blum's single-mindedness meant he would do whatever he wished if he believed his actions were right. It would be the pattern of his life.

How Blum got his Name

IT WAS MY first day at school. In the yard between the Victorian building and the cottage where our schoolmistress lived, I waited for the bell to sound the start of my state education. Girls whispered to each other and giggled. Bigger boys pushed and shoved each other and shouted and laughed. I stood apart; a watcher, an outsider, I knew nobody.

Then I noticed another lad with new shoes, grey shorts and long socks, who also stood apart from the other thirty-odd children. Unlike me, his attention was directed not at the others, but upwards. He moved to one side, peered up into the big elm tree in the corner. He shielded his eyes with one hand to blot out September sun.

He dropped his gaze, looked about, as though he wanted to share something. Nobody seemed to be aware of him, but he caught my eye, pointed up into the elm. I looked, but saw nothing. He jerked his head; he wanted me to join him. I moved between two girls who were skipping and two lads squabbling over the tangled strings of their tin yo-yos.

He pointed upwards as I joined him, 'There's an owl up there.'

I couldn't see anything. I'd never seen an owl, not in real life, only in pictures.

I felt stupid. All I could see was a tree, 'Where?'

He poked his finger upwards. His voice had a hint of irritation. 'Smack up against the trunk. On the big branch, left hand side. There.'

Still I couldn't see anything. The other boy made a hissing noise. Straight away, as it turned its head, opened its yellow eyes, I could see. 'It's a Tawny, a brown owl,' he said, 'It'll be roosting up there.'

I watched the owl as it closed its eyes and swivelled its head away. 'I've never seen one.'

He looked at me. 'What? -- Never?' I shook my head. He turned away, in apparent disgust. We continued to stare at the dozing owl.

The sound of a bell intruded. I turned as Mrs. Beattie, our headmistress, appeared at the porch ringing a wooden-handled brass bell. Children stopped what they were doing, began to file inside. My companion, though, ignored the bell and Mrs. Beattie's presence. He pointed at the owl.

'If it roosts up there regular, like, it should've spewed up some pellets,' he said, 'I'll show yer.'

He made a move towards the trunk of the elm.

I was torn between this boy's offer to show me something I knew nothing about and the authority figure holding the bell.

'You boys -- That includes you two, as well,' called Mrs. Beattie, 'Come along, and hurry up.'

The authority figure won. She stood aside and I hurried in, but lingered in the porch, just behind her by the row of pot sinks, that smelt of carbolic soap. My companion, though, took his time.

He jerked his thumb over his shoulder as he ambled towards Mrs. Beattie, 'There's a brown owl up there, missus.'

'It's Mrs. Beattie, or Miss, to you David Gatley. And you're not here to look at owls,' she said, 'Inside.--. Quickly, now.'

The school was split into three rooms. The classroom for five to seven-year-olds was at the back. The room for seven to eleven-year-olds was at the front. In-between was the Big Room, a place with two fireplaces, the venue for morning prayers and where two long tables were each day set for mid-day dinner. There were no indoor lavatories and you had to cross either the girls' or boys' separate playgrounds to visit the earth closet toilets, or 'the bogs' as we soon knew them.

For the next two years we would be taught to read, write and do sums by Mrs. Beattie. Afterwards, we would move to Miss. Hetty Hothersall's class. There we would be brow-beaten into 11 Plus cannon fodder in an endless, repetitive cycle of English language, mental arithmetic and simple mathematics, leavened by a smattering of history, geography and nature study. She kept order with her sharp tongue and, if needed, a mahogany ruler which didn't often leave her hand.

Our first sight of Miss. Hothersall was at morning prayers. She looked far from threatening as she sang with gusto and played hymns on the piano while the vicar, Dr Snipe, read from the Bible, led our prayers, and welcomed us newcomers with a speech he must have repeated each autumn term for decades.

On that first morning, after prayers, Mrs. Beattie allocated our desks and issued us with pencils and an exercise book apiece. I was pleased to sit next to David Gatley, until now the only other pupil who had spoken to me. Mrs. Beattie set her older pupils some work and gave us newcomers a talk on school rules.

I listened, but was aware David Gatley was far from interested. He was bored. He fidgeted and fiddled with everything in his reach, obviously ill at ease, as Mrs. Beattie told us we must not speak to others in class, we must not go outside the front gate before home-time, we must put up our hand before we addressed her as 'Miss.' or 'Mrs. Beattie.' The rules seemed endless. She finished on the matter of toilets.

'If you need the toilets, you must put your hand up and ask, "Please may I cross the yard?"'

She moved on to the alphabet and chalked the letters, in capitals and lower case, on the blackboard. She was gauging how much each of us newcomers knew. In turn we tried to recite it for her, some with more confidence and success than others. At quarter past eleven we stopped for break -- or 'lunch' as it was oddly called.

Mrs. Beattie herded us through to the Big Room and handed out our free milk, one third of a pint bottle each, courtesy of the new post-war welfare state. The others took their milk and a single paper straw from a cardboard carton and drank it with relish. I put my straw in the bottle and tried to drink, but even the smell made me queasy. I never touched milk in my youth and even now can't stomach it neat.

I could see nowhere to hide it, or even pour it away, without being caught. I looked at David Gatley as his straw made a guttering sound in the dregs of his milk. He put his empty in the crate, moved to the tall glass-fronted bookcase full of fossils, stuffed birds, a world globe, and other curiosities. I followed him as he looked into the bookcase we later found out was referred to by the grand title of school museum.

I checked over my shoulder. Mrs. Beattie was talking to three girls. I whispered to David Gatley, 'Do you want my milk?' He looked at me, surprised. I kept my voice low, 'It makes me feel sick.'

He nodded, took my bottle. He drained most of it in one suck. He waved the bottle towards the bookcase. Next to the world globe was a stuffed bird with a long beak and gleaming black eyes. Its dusty feathers were blue and its breast orange. It was perched on a twig anchored in a disc of varnished wood. 'I bet you don't know what that is.'

I shook my head.

'Bet you haven't seen one alive and all.'

I shook my head.

'I have,' he said, 'There's two pair on the cut past Jackson's bridge. I've seen 'em many a time with me dad.'

He peered at the bird. 'It's a kingfisher. I hate seeing 'em stuffed. It's not right.'

He sucked the rest of the milk from the bottle. 'If we were up there now we'd see kingfishers all right.' He handed back my empty bottle. 'We can't though, not stuck in 'ere.'

Back in the classroom we returned to the alphabet. It was a warm day and we were told we could take off our jerseys if we wished. Now and then I looked towards David Gatley as he fidgeted, moving his pencil this way and that on the slope of the desk. He stopped abruptly, put up his hand.

'Can I cross the yard?' he said.

Mrs Beattie continued telling us about letters, words and the English language. David Gatley waved his hand.

'I want to go to the...'

Mrs Beattie cut him off, 'You mustn't interrupt. Put your hand up and wait.'

His tone was impatient, 'I just want to go to the lav!'

There were one or two sniggers, cut short by Mrs. Beattie's stern looks.

She pointed at David Gatley, 'You put your hand up, wait for me, and then say "Please, may I cross the yard?"'

He looked about, avoided her gaze. She snapped, 'Look at me, David Gatley.'

With a sigh, he faced her.

'Now, you say it,' said Mrs. Beattie.

He hesitated, then in a sing-song tone, on the edge of insolence, said, 'Please may I cross the yard?'

She nodded and David Gatley left his desk, went out through the back porch. We didn't see him again for an hour.

After five minutes, or so, Mrs Beattie sent one of the older boys, Glyn Ormesher, to fetch him from the bogs. Glyn came back and announced he couldn't find him. 'I looked in all the privies, Miss.'

These days there would be an immediate call to the police and a wide scale search. On that morning, Mrs. Beattie remained calm at the news, but used the occasion for a warning.

'Let me say this now. Anyone who goes across the yard and doesn't come straight back will be punished. Do you hear me?'

'Yes, Miss.' we said in unison.

The next time we saw David Gatley was when he was pushed into the classroom by a woman I'd never seen before. Her face was flushed, 'I'm sorry, Mrs. Beattie. I don't know what he thinks he's up to. I found him in our garden.'

Murmurings travelled around the room. David Gatley's errant behaviour had impressed, shocked or amused my classmates. Mrs. Beattie hushed them with a bark, 'Silence, please!'

She turned to the woman, 'Leave it to me, thank you Mrs. Gatley.'

Mrs. Gatley backed away, 'I'm very sorry.'

'Back to your place, David Gatley' said Mrs. Beattie, 'I'll deal with you later.'

David Gatley went back to his desk. Mrs. Gatley paused at the door. She masked her embarrassment with a glare at her son. 'Wait 'til your father hears about this.'

When dinnertime arrived and we queued to wash our hands with carbolic soap, Mrs. Beattie kept David Gatley back from the Big Room. I was already sitting at one of the long tables with a plate of minced beef pie and a dollop of mash and boiled cabbage, when he came out of our classroom, followed by Mrs. Beattie, who told him to sit down. He looked around and pushed in at the table between me and a girl wearing pink health service specs. Mrs. Beattie spoke to a dinner lady and she brought him his plate.

I was curious, 'What did Mrs. Beattie say?'

'Nowt, much, but she give me a right wallop on me leg,' he rolled to one side, knocking the girl with the specs' elbow.

'Don't do that', she said, but was ignored by David Gatley, who displayed a red weal across the back of his lower thigh.

'Did it hurt?' I said.

'Nah.' He turned to his plate. He took his knife and fork, picked up his slice of pie and flipped it across on to my plate, 'Swaps for your cow juice, don't like mince.'

After dinner, Mrs. Beattie took me aside. I wondered which rule I'd broken, fearing a similar stripe on my leg, but she told me if David Gatley asked to go across the yard, I must go with him.

'What if I don't want to go, Miss?' I said.

She suppressed her exasperation, 'It doesn't matter. Just go with him and make sure he doesn't go home again. Do you understand?'

I nodded and thought no more of it.

Back in the classroom it was even hotter than earlier. Through the tall windows the clear blue sky and the bright sunshine made inside with its dull green walls seem gloomy. While Mrs. Beattie told us about how ancient people created and developed writing, I noticed David Gatley using his pencil to wiggle a staple from the spine of his exercise book. He tore a piece of paper from an inside page and folded it around the staple. Then he tucked it into the top of his sock. I was intrigued.

A short time later, he raised his hand and waved it. I remembered my instructions as Mrs. Beattie paused and looked at him. 'May I cross the yard?' he said.

Mrs Beattie gave him a pointed prompt, '*Please*, may I cross the yard?'

He repeated her prompt. As David Gatley got up, Mrs. Beattie caught my eye, nodded to me. I felt the curious eyes of the class on me as I stood as well. With my face reddening, I followed him out.

David Gatley wandered out across the cinder schoolyard, but he didn't go to the bogs. He leaned on the back wall, looked out over the parish hall field, where dozens of butterflies criss-crossed each other's paths. Birds were singing. Beyond the rough grass, field after field of barley stubble were hazed by September heat. I could see the hump-back of Billy's bridge a quarter of a mile away and a glimpse of the canal reflecting the sunlight. Further away still was the blurred green rise of Clieves Hill at Aughton. I walked towards David Gatley. I could hear bees and on the air was the stink of manure.

He looked at me as I joined him, turned back to the view.

'What are you doing?' I said.

'Watching a skylark.'

I looked out across the field, 'Where is it?'

'Up in the sky. Where do you think?'

I felt as stupid as I did when he showed me the owl.

'Where?'

'Can you see the bridge?

'Yeah.'

'Look at the bridge, 'he said and pointed his finger. 'Then straight up from there and you'll see it. It looks dead titchy from here.'

I did as he said and saw the tiny speck of a bird mounting higher. Though it was a long way away, I could hear its tinkling song.

'It's my dad's favourite bird,' he said, as he climbed onto the low wall and slid into the field.

He'd stepped outside the school boundary. I felt a spark of concern; it was against the rules, or at least going outside the gate was, 'I thought you wanted a wee?'

'Nah.'

Concern turned to panic as he moved away, 'You're not going home again, are you?' He shook his head, moved to a straggle of bramble and started to pick blackberries. He thumbed them into his mouth, offered me one. I took it and crushed it with my tongue. We'd had sweet custard with our treacle pudding at dinner and the berry tasted tart in comparison.

'There's some pears along there,' he said, nodding along the hedge which ran eighty yards to the canal by Lolly's bridge, on the road that passed the school. He ambled towards the pears and I pulled myself up on the wall for a better look. Branches heavy with fruit dipped over the hedge from a house next to the school. I slung my legs over the wall and dropped into the field to join him.

He reached up and picked two pears, stuffing one into each pocket of his short trousers. 'Do you go fishing on the cut?' he said.

'My mum won't let me. She says it's dangerous.'

'Ha, I go with me dad.' He paused a moment, then added, 'You'll have to come with us.'

I was about to ask when we could go, but he stared into the middle distance and drummed his fingers on his head. After a moment, he stopped this odd mannerism.

'Get a pear and I'll show you something.'

He set off along the hedge. I plucked a pear and followed. Next to the garden was a paddock. David Gatley approached it and clicked his tongue. I was amazed to see a pony trot straight to him. He rubbed its nose, fed it a pear. 'You give him one now,' he said.

I held up the pear and the pony moved towards me.

'Don't let him eat it in one go. Just give us a minute.'

He leaned over the fence as I let the pony bite at the pear. The pony crunched the hard fruit and David Gatley reached for its hindquarters and pulled at its tail. The pony jerked away, but the pear was too much to resist. I held it out of its reach. My companion again reached for its tail.

'All right, he can have it now,' he said.

I let the pony take the pear as David Gatley beamed and held up strands of hair from its tail.

'Did that hurt him?'

'Ha, he didn't feel a thing.'

'What's it for?'

'I'll show yer,' he said and ran along the hedge. I hesitated a moment. Mrs. Beattie did tell me not to let him go home. But he wasn't going home. He told me he wasn't. I felt a burst of exhilaration as I ran through the long grass after him, leaving school behind.

I reached the edge of the canal to see him kicking at clumps of grass on the towpath. He loosened one then pulled at it with his hands. He turned over the sod and picked out an earthworm. He dropped the sod and produced a clean handkerchief from his pocket.

'Dig up some more and stick 'em in this.'

While I pulled out more sods and collected another couple of worms, I kept an eye on him. He retrieved the folded paper from his sock, took out the staple and used his teeth to twist it open. Then he took a length of horsehair and again used his teeth to clamp the staple to its tip.

'Give us a worm.'

He took a worm and impaled it on the staple. He displayed it to me as it thrashed and squirmed at this sudden, violent change to its existence.

'Watch this.'

He knelt at the edge of the canal on the wide slabs of stone which guided the towpath under the bridge. I got down beside him as he lowered the worm into the water at the edge of the cut. The wriggling worm went out of sight into dark green water.

After a moment he raised the horsehair half an inch at a time. As the worm came back into view, two sticklebacks attacked it like a pair of dogs.

'You got to be careful now,' he said. 'Wait for one to get hold on the worm and…'

He whipped the horsehair out on to the stones. A stickleback flashed silver in the sunlight. It had gorged half the worm. He turned to me, 'Want a go?'

I couldn't wait. He pulled the fish off the worm, dropped it back in the water, handed me the horsehair. I copied his example and lowered the worm into the water and out of sight.

'Jack sharps are dead greedy and they'll near choke 'emselves getting hold of the worm.'

I raised the horsehair and seconds later had a glittering jack sharp in my hand. I knelt and admired it. The thrill of pure pleasure was like nothing I'd felt before. To be in this, to me, forbidden place, treasure in my hand, made me feel my life had clicked into gear. But the moment was broken by the whoops of boys and a voice that shouted, 'Down there. Let's gerrem!'

On the track from the top of the bridge down to the towpath, four older boys from Hetty Hothersall's junior class charged down to us. They stopped short, but a stocky lad I later knew as Norman Buckleigh stepped forward as their self-styled leader.

'Mrs. Beattie sent us to fetch you back,'

'Let's dip 'em in the cut first, eh?' jeered a skinny boy called Trevor Hurst. He moved towards me and grabbed my shirt front. I was startled.

'Not today, Hurstie, 'Buckleigh said, 'We're taking them straight back,' He put a hand on David Gatley's shoulder.

David Gatley swiped Buckleigh's hand off, 'We're doing nowt wrong.'

'Don't be a prannet,' said Buckleigh, 'You're wanted back. Nowt you can do about it.'

Buckleigh and his group herded us back to school, predicted all sorts of nasty consequences for going AWOL. We were met by a furious Mrs. Beattie. This was when I found out punishment at our school was often a public event. Mrs. Beattie stood us in front of the class and tongue-lashed us for our irresponsible behaviour. Then she made us turn around and pull up the hems of our shorts.

She took a ruler from a cupboard and struck David Gatley on his right leg. I heard the slap and flinched as the class gasped. Then she hit my right leg; the same reaction from our classmates. A third swish connected with David Gatley's left leg and the a fourth hit my own. It hurt, but neither of us cried out, or cried.

We were sent back to our desks and as we gabbled through the home time prayer, despite the pain and embarrassment, I felt a sort of pride. I had joined the roll of dishonour by being one of the few who got the ruler on their first day. David Gatley had become a school folk hero, a legend, for getting it twice.

Next morning I couldn't wait to go to school, if only to see my new friend. We went into prayers together then afterwards went to our desks. I was surprised to see another new boy, Michael Millican, sitting at my desk. I protested he was in my place, but Mrs. Beattie intervened and pointed to my new seat, two across from my former desk. I realised David Gatley and me were being kept apart.

Later that morning, David Gatley put up his hand and said, 'Can I go across the yard?' Michael Millican shot up like a jack-in-the-box.

Mrs. Beattie said, 'Not yet, Michael.' I realised I'd also been replaced in my role as David Gatley's keeper.

She turned to David Gatley and said, 'Aren't you forgetting something?'

David Gatley sat defiant, as all eyes settled on him.

Mrs. Beattie said, 'Can anyone tell me what he should say?'

The girl with the pink specs was eager. Her hand shot up, 'Miss, Miss!'

Mrs. Beattie gave her the nod, 'Go on Rosemary.'

She lisped, *'Please*, may I go across the yard?'

'Thank you, Rosemary,' said Mrs. Beattie, 'Well, David Gatley?'

There was a silence. Everyone watched him. His face went red. Still, he said nothing. I could hear the big clock above the fireplace.

Tick-tock.

'I'm waiting,' said Mrs. Beattie.

We all waited. David Gatley chewed at his cheek, twisted in his seat, pursed his lips and folded his arms around himself.

Mrs. Beattie folded her arms as well, as determined as her pupil to save face, 'Well?'

The seconds continued to tick past.

Then, in a burst of frustration that he had to conform, to toe the line, he let it out, almost an angry shout, 'Please may I go across the blummin' yard!'

Laughter erupted. There was uproar. To close it down, Mrs. Beattie had to shout. David Gatley turned right and left to grin at our classmates. Mrs. Beattie was outraged. David Gatley got the ruler for the third time. It was the day Blum Gatley earned his nickname. He would be known by that name for the rest of his life.

End-of-Term Prizes

IT WAS TWILIGHT when we climbed over the back wall of the churchyard. I told my mum and dad I wanted to fish late to catch a carp. Blum gave his mam the same story. In fact, we were about to become burglars for the first time.

Of course, Blum didn't see it like that. He was excited, single-minded, he knew what he wanted. I was scared.

It didn't help that we were walking between graves. I told myself I didn't believe in ghosts, but still I tried not to look at the names on the gravestones, just in case it was possible to disturb any restless souls. I was also afraid we might be caught. Blum assured me we wouldn't. To achieve his desire would be what he called 'a blummin' doddle.'

With pipistrelle bats fluttering before us in the thickening dusk, we threaded between the graves to our first challenge -- the high wall of the vicarage garden.

Blum laid his fishing tackle at the foot of the wall and gave himself a leg-up on a stained, white marble headstone. I tried not to look at the owner's name, but I couldn't help myself. I read the words at top speed -- 'Ellen Sossin, loving wife of Albert Sossin' -- then whipped my eyes away. Blum sat astride the high wall, whispered to me to do the same.

The plan was to climb the wall and use it as a footway to enter the vicarage via its back yard and garden, but I hesitated. I felt uneasy treating this dead woman's headstone like a stepladder. It seemed wrong. Was Ellen Sossin aware of us? Was she a restless soul? Would she sense our dishonest intent and appear to frighten us, force us to flee? The thought made me shiver.

Blum's voice was low and urgent, 'Come on, it's easy.'

I dumped my tackle with Blum's and moved towards Ellen Sossin's gravestone. At that moment, I heard the sound of a motor. Blum slid from the top of the wall to crouch atop Ellen's headstone. We froze. A vehicle approached and braked. The engine was switched off.

We heard the door open and close. Blum raised himself and looked over the vicarage wall. He put his finger to his lips, gestured for me to climb up on Ellen's stone. My legs shook as I pushed myself upward and peered over the top of the wall.

The vehicle was a dark coloured car. Alongside it stood a man wearing overalls and a flat cap. I didn't recognise his face, even when he struck a match to light a cigarette.

I whispered, 'Who is it?'

Blum shook his head then spoke low. 'Like his car, mind, Zephyr Estate, '56.'

The man paced up and down for a minute or more. He dragged on his fag as though trying to finish it quickly. I could smell the burning tobacco in the still, damp air. Then came the headlights of another vehicle. Its lights were switched off as a large vehicle drew up behind the Zephyr.

'Can't see what that one is,' whispered Blum.

The waiting man tossed away his cigarette as the doors of the second vehicle opened and two men got out to join him. They stood on the vicarage driveway, spoke in low voices. Blum's voice was a murmur, 'We'll have to wait.'

'Can't we leave it 'til tomorrow?'

'Why should we? They're not going to stand there blummin' gassing all night.'

My legs were shaking even more now and I wanted to go home. Perched on Ellen Sossin's headstone, I thought back on what had happened that day. Why were we here when I'd sooner be watching the telly? Or even trying to catch a carp? It had been a day unlike any other I'd known.

*

WE WERE IN Hetty Hothersall's class at that time. It was the year before the 11 Plus. It was a muggy July day two weeks ahead of the summer holidays. For me, and for Blum, the long break couldn't come soon enough.

We were about to tackle the dreaded 'Twenty Mental;' in other words, twenty mental arithmetic questions. On other afternoons, we had only ten. That was bad enough, but twenty was a Friday ordeal. Hetty was about to ask the first question when our headmistress, Mrs. Beattie, entered, apologised for her interruption, and hiding her mouth behind her hand, whispered to Hetty.

Hetty turned to the class and said, 'Twelve times table, please, while I'm out of the room.'

'One- twelve- is- twelve,' prompted Hetty then followed Mrs. Beattie, as she withdrew to the Big Room.

The goodie-goodies at once started to chant, 'One- twelve- is- twelve, two- twelves-twenty-four…'

I didn't bother. I hated numbers, maths, everything about them. To chant times tables without a teacher in the room was unthinkable. I looked across at Blum and caught his eye. His face confirmed his disgust. We remained silent. The others reached twelve-times-twelve and looked at each other for guidance in the absence of Hetty. The voice of Gillian Sumner commanded the room. She was posh and wore glasses and her dad was an accountant in Southport. She never did anything wrong.

'One twelve is twelve,' Gillian reprised in her bossy voice and the class followed her example. The table was repeated three times, but Blum and I joined in only when Hetty came back into the room. Even though the chanted times table was unfinished, she raised the ruler which seldom left her hand. The class became silent.

She pointed the ruler at me, then Blum, 'You two go to the Big Room and see Mrs. Beattie.'

There was a murmur of hushed speculation from our classmates.

Hetty quelled it in an instant, 'Quiet!'

Blum and I swapped a quick look. Our thoughts were the same: why us? I was apprehensive, my mind running back over recent misdemeanours. Who'd snitched on us? Why did she want us when we were about to do Twenty Mental? Did she somehow know we hadn't joined in to chant the twelve times table?

Hetty eyed me as I left the room, followed by Blum. My apprehension budged up a notch or two.

*

FIVE MINUTES LATER we were breaking the school rule of exiting the front gate between nine and half-past-three, but with the authority of the headmistress herself. I wondered if we were chosen only for the reason we were both no-hopers when it came to 'mental' and our contributions would not be missed.

I carried a cardboard Crosse and Blackwell baked beans box and Blum a carton printed Heinz Salad Cream. Each contained books earmarked for end-of-summer-term school prizes for the goodie-goodies, all to be inscribed by the vicar, Dr Snipe. Mine contained also an envelope addressed to him in Mrs. Beattie's neat handwriting, no doubt instructions to him on what to write inside each winner's prize book.

For a few moments I wondered if there was a prize for me, but put the thought away as wishful thinking. I concentrated on the bliss of being out of class on this stifling afternoon. Our destination, the vicarage, was more than half-a- mile away and by the time we returned from our errand, Twenty

Mental wouldn't concern us again for a full week. We were chuffed.

To the rumble of faraway thunder, I strode forward breathing in the scent of honeysuckle from the parish hall hedge. Along the roadside, a thousand stalks of cow parsley stretched into the distance, their blossoms like endless blobs of cream. I could hear skylarks and a missel thrush, perched on a telegraph pole, sang to predict a possible thunderstorm.

'Don't walk so fast,' said Blum, 'If we don't rush we won't be back 'til home-time.'

I laughed, slowed down. I hadn't thought of that.

We passed the Scottish Soldier pub with its roof of reed thatch and through the trees I could make-out the tower of the abbey. Everyone called it that, but it was a wealthy family's private chapel that was never finished after Henry the Eighth put the boot in on the Roman Catholic Church and its supporters. It fascinated me, but I'd never been inside the jungle of blackthorn, elder and briars that hid its ruins from the road.

'When we've seen Dr Snipe we could sneak in and have a look,' said Blum, 'Billy Hurst says you can climb right up the tower if you know what you're doing.'

'Has he done it?'

'Don't care if he has' Blum shrugged, 'We can do it if we want.'

Anything seemed possible that afternoon.

We walked up the drive at the vicarage, keen to finish our errand and enjoy this unexpected helping of freedom.

It was a huge house, too big for a man on his own like Dr Snipe. People were often confused why he was called doctor, but once Mrs. Beattie told us he was a notable scholar as well as a vicar, not a dispenser of penicillin and vaccinations. He was the son of an Anglican Bishop from the south of England.

We knew him only as an old duffer, a kind and gentle man, but out of touch with us youngsters and modern life. He didn't visit school often now. We both remembered last autumn after harvest festival when he brought the traditional boxes of fruit to the school to give each boy and girl an apple and a pear from the vicarage gardens. Mrs. Beattie had to stop him as he smiled and nodded, handed out rotten fruit. We heard he'd mislaid the decent fruit and picked up decaying windfalls from the vicarage garden. About the same time, Blum's mam told us members of the congregation had complained that Dr Snipe allowed snot to drip from his nose into the communion wine. On behalf of the outraged members of the congregation, Captain Westbrook wrote to the Bishop of Liverpool requesting urgent action in the form of his removal, but Dr Snipe was still our vicar.

Blum yanked the iron rod which hung by the front door. From inside we heard a bell jangle. We waited a few minutes, but nobody answered. Dr Snipe was not married, but we knew Mrs. Bartlett cleaned for the vicar and made his dinner, but Blum thought she was only there mornings. I pulled the bell rod again. Two minutes, or so passed and there was still no answer. Blum hammered on the door without result. I pushed at the door, but it was locked or bolted.

'We'll have to go round the blummin' back,' said Blum.

We went around the side of the house where a walled garden adjoined the churchyard. The half-acre of garden must once have been impressive. Now, the lawns were in poor condition with overgrown edges. Couch grass had invaded flower beds and the box hedges needed cutting back and re-shaping. Neglected fruit trees stood in a sea of seeding grass, docks, thistles and yellow ragwort. Willow herb, groundsel and shepherd's purse occupied almost every crack in the back yard paving. The air was still and heavy; a distant aeroplane droned, but the loudest sounds were the buzz of bees and zizz of grasshoppers.

I knocked on the back door, but rather than wait, Blum turned the ring latch and the door opened.

Confident with the authority of our headmistress, we went inside, through a vestibule, past Dr Snipe's old tweed overcoat hung on a nail, into the kitchen.

Blum called from the deserted kitchen, 'Dr Snipe?'

'Anyone home?' I shouted. The stillness of the house seemed to swallow our voices. We plonked the boxes on a long table where a single place was set. Between knife and fork was a plate of boiled ham with hard-boiled eggs and sliced tomatoes under a domed, mesh fly protector. I could smell pipe tobacco and coffee.

'Dr Snipe?' Blum called again.

I waited a moment and shouted, 'Hello?'

There was no reply.

'I wonder if he's got his deaf aid on,' I said.

'Let's just dump them and go.'

'We could, but...'

'He'll find them as soon as he gets back.'

'Mrs. Beattie said she rang him up and told us we'd deliver them to him. You know, personal.'

Blum blew out, in irritation, 'What are we supposed to do? Search the house 'til we find him?'

'It's better than telling Mrs. Beattie we just dumped them.'

'I thought you wanted to go to the abbey before we went back?'

'Yeah, but she did say to wait for any reply.'

Blum sighed, 'Right, but let's do it quick.'

He headed for the inner door and pushed it open, calling for Dr Snipe. It led into a narrow back hall then into a big front hallway. Near the door ticked a fancy long case clock with a dial of painted flowers. A curved stairway rose to a landing with spindled balustrades and big, old pictures. Off the hallway were several doors. Dull, stained wallpaper peeled from above the skirting boards. A big Turkey rug was so worn and grubby it looked like sacking. A Bakelite telephone squatted on a small table in the hall beside an oak monk's bench which was piled with open box files, parish newsletters and correspondence, all testaments to the chaos of Dr Snipe's parish work.

Blum went to the foot of the stairs and again shouted for Dr. Snipe. Still, there was no response.

I went to the door closest to me and knocked. I opened it and looked in. I called Dr Snipe's name again, as I went inside. Between the long windows and a huge fireplace were two sofas and several armchairs. There were books piled everywhere. Close to the fireplace a winged, leather armchair stood with its back towards me. On a side table lay a blackened briar pipe and a leather tobacco pouch. I wondered again if the vicar had removed his deaf aid and I stepped forward and peered round the chair expecting to find him reading, perhaps asleep, but the chair was empty.

Knuckles rapped on wood as Blum called yet again for Dr Snipe. I left the room as he turned the knob of another door off the hallway. I joined him as he pushed it open. We stood open-mouthed at sight of the interior. It was obvious that it was untouched by Mrs. Bartlett's cleaning regime. I'd never seen such a dusty and cluttered room.

We looked at each other and stepped inside. It was as big as the sitting room I'd entered a minute earlier, but its tall windows were covered by canvas blinds, that restricted the daylight. Shelves lined the high walls from ceiling to floor. Most were filled with books and sheaves of papers. Others housed what looked like pieces of stone. Even the bare floorboards were almost hidden by towers of books, boxes and files. Opposite the fire place was a big desk piled with more books and bundles of papers. A leather captain's chair, its seat worn and cracked, was pushed half away from the desk, as if abandoned minutes ago, but there was no sign of the vicar.

Blum took in the room, snorted, 'Ha, it's like a blummin' junk shop.'

On the vicar's desk, in the small space among piles of papers, was a book lying open. The text was unlike anything I'd seen before. Only much later did I realise it was Hebrew, or Aramaic, or another ancient language. Alongside it was a handwritten letter stuffed half- back inside an envelope. addressed to the vicarage. Apart from a fine covering of dust, it looked like it had been opened that day, but the postmark read 'Paddington, December 14, 1947.' Under it was another letter in the same hand. The postmark read 'Oxford, January 23, 1948.' I wondered how often the vicar visited this room.

'Come on, let's find him,' I said, my voice hushed. But Blum was too busy looking around to take any notice.

He picked up a stone from a shelf and weighed it in his hand. He turned it over.

'Hand axe,' he said.

I was curious, 'What?'

He indicated a paper label gummed to the rock, 'That's what it says on here.' He pushed it back on the shelf, 'Doesn't look like a blummin' hatchet to me.'

He picked up another similar, but smaller piece of rock and examined it. 'Nowt on this one.'

He moved on along the room. My eye was caught by a small pile of what looked like tiles. Our reason for being there now forgotten, I took one from the top of the pile. It was covered in dust, but I could feel and see it was clay. I blew at the dust. On one side were carved odd shapes and marks I didn't understand. I turned it over to see a label, 'Sokce Gozu, Gaziantep, 1908.'

I put the tile back and moved along the shelf, fascinated. I saw beads, also made of clay, pieces of broken pottery and plates and bowls of metal, some of which were green and mouldy-looking like old copper pipe fittings. A label on a piece of pottery read, 'Samarra, Mesopotamia, 1911.'

Blum interrupted, 'Look at this. It's old Snipey years ago.'

I left the shelf, joined him. He pointed at a framed photograph on the wall of a young man and woman with a man in Arab dress. She is smiling. Her fine featured face is radiant; she is beautiful.

'You can see it's Snipey, but younger,' said Blum, 'Looks like he was in the army, in Africa, or somewhere.'

Blum moved away as I examined the photo. It is definitely Dr Snipe. He wears long shorts and a solar topee hat as well as a military-type shirt with epaulettes. He smiles as he holds a cigarette close to his face. The young woman wears a long skirt and boots and a similar shirt. She is shorter than him and turns half towards him, looking up, sharing in whatever makes him smile. Doctor Snipe's other hand rests on the Arab man's shoulder. The Arab smiles at the camera, displaying the gaps of half a dozen missing teeth.

There were other photos. One showed Dr Snipe looking on as the same woman bandages a child's foot. Another showed Dr Snipe and the woman sitting on a cane sofa together reading a newspaper. The headlines were in some foreign language like French. A man in long Arab dress and a fez hat pours coffee or tea from a tall pot with a spout like a swan's neck. A third photograph shows Dr Snipe, an arm around the young woman's shoulders. A score or more of dirty, but smiling, excited Arab children surround them. The woman holds hands with a small girl. Dr Snipe has a tobacco pipe in his mouth, but I still recognise his now rarely-seen smile.

I moved to the next photo. Dr Snipe stands by a lake or river. In one hand he has a fishing rod. In the other he holds high a trio of large fish, strung together with a cord through their gills. The Arab with the missing teeth holds up a similar bundle as he grins at the camera.

But it is the next photograph that thrills me. On a summer's day like this, the young Dr Snipe, clad in a blazer and a straw boater hat, stands on the lawn before the brick and flint wall of a country house with an older man. He wears old-fashioned clothes. His hair is parted down the middle, he has a bushy moustache. He passes a book to the young Dr Snipe. Both men have a hand on the book. Both smile.

I peered at the bottom of the frame at the hand-written caption, *'With Jerome K. Jerome, Oxfordshire, 1910.'*

I flushed with excitement. Did Dr Snipe know Jerome K. Jerome? Is the book in the photograph *Three Men in a Boat*? Since I was seven years old I had read and re-read my father's old copy of the book which had never been out of print since Victorian times. I stared at the photograph, but my eyes were drawn lower to the shelf beneath them. I realised straight away the blurred gold titling of the book in the photograph was there before me, lying on a morocco leather blotter.

The noise of Blum as he moved about the room exploring its contents receded as I reached for the book. I opened it, transfixed by the vivid, marbled end-papers. Then turned its pages at random and smiled at the drawing of Uncle Podger hanging the picture. I turned more pages and discovered a plain postcard once posted to an address in Bayswater, London. I took it out and put the book aside. I turned over the card with trembling hands. Its hand-written note in faded ink was headed 'Ewelme, Oxon, July 28, 1910.'

All awareness of my surroundings deserted me as I read, *'Dear Crispin, It was good of you and your parents to visit Ettie and me. I enjoyed our talk about your time at Oxford and first experiences of your new profession. I must say I don't recall having met another young man who could quote from T.M.I.A.B. verbatim! It was my pleasure to sign your copy. Ettie says you must come for tea again and bring your fiancée Dora! Ettie will send the photograph soonest. Do write. Best wishes to His Grace and Mrs. Snipe. Yours, fondly, JKJ.'*

I riffled back to the title page, found the handwritten inscription. 'For my young friend, Crispin Snipe, a valued reader, Best regards, Jerome K. Jerome, July 1910.'

I blurted out in my excitement, 'This is my favourite book and our vicar knew the man who wrote it!'

I became aware of my surroundings again. 'Blum, look!'

He appeared from behind a tall bookcase with something in his hand.

I brandished the book at him. 'This book, it's signed by Jerome K. Jerome. The vicar knew him! Look!'

But Blum ignored me. Jerome K. Jerome meant nothing to him, though I had now and then spoken of the book's funniest bits. He held up three sticks of hexagonal split-bamboo; a fishing rod. He in turn was excited.

'Fancy old Snipey having this!' he said.

'There's a picture of him fishing,' I said, but I was more concerned with the book. I pushed it towards him, pointed at the inscription, 'Look, JKJ signed it.'

Blum spoke over me, displayed the butt section, 'Look at this. Know what it is?'

He held up the sections, jabbing his finger at the lettering beneath the varnish above the cork grip,

'It's a Hardy -- A blummin' Roach Perfection. It says on it!'

He held the rod, his eyes glittering, admiring it, his fingers touching the silvery rings and maroon silk whippings that fastened them to the varnished cane.

'It's like the one in the photo,' I said.

I pointed to the framed picture. He pushed his face up against the image, examined it, and then squinted as he compared it with the rod butt in his hand.

'It is,' he said, 'It's the same rod. What are these fish? They're a bit like chub, but…What's this place?'

I looked at the caption, read it aloud: '"Tigris salmon", The Tigris, 1912.'

'They're not blummin' salmon,' Blum scoffed and pointed, 'Look at them two. Some sort of carp or other, a chub, I reckon.'

I wanted him to appreciate my pleasure in finding the book, 'Did you hear what I said about this?'

He propped the rod sections against the wall and took the book, still open at the inscription and looked at it. 'What about it?'

'The vicar must have known Jerome K. Jerome. He was dead famous -- still is. I wish I could ask him about it.'

'Ask him then,' said Blum. He handed back the book, picked up the rod, lost in his own, matching enthusiasm, 'I wonder if he'd let me have a go of this.'

The telephone in the hall started to ring. We froze for a moment as it continued, then looked at each other.

'I bet its Mrs. Beattie. She'll want to know where we are,' I said.

Blum hurried to put the rod back. I put the postcard inside the book, replaced it on the blotter. The telephone rang on.

'Come on, before he comes to answer it,' Blum said as he moved to the door. I followed and we peered out through the crack of the open door. The telephone continued to ring. We sidled into the hallway and closed the door behind us.

'Dr Snipe?' Blum called. We both adopted a casual air of innocence.

'Hello? Anyone home?' I called, to add to the illusion.

The telephone stopped ringing.

'I'm fed up of this,' said Blum, 'We're wasting time. Let's get on with it before Mrs. Beattie sends someone to find us.'

We each shouted again for Dr Snipe. Then Blum moved to the monk's bench. He held up the battery case, wires and earpiece of the vicar's deaf aid. 'No wonder he can't hear the blummin' phone, or owt else.'

He lowered it back into the clutter.

'You go upstairs and I'll have a look in the other rooms. He could be up the lane or sat in the flippin' garden.'

He moved off, heading back to the kitchen, again calling for Dr Snipe. I hurried upstairs shouting the vicar's name.

I could hear Blum's calls as I knocked on the first door upstairs and looked in. All I saw was a bed. Shouting for the vicar as I went to the next door, which was ajar. I peeped in, saw a sofa and wardrobe. Beyond them was an inner door, also half open. I called Dr Snipe again, but this time my voice was lower. Framed in the second doorway was an old-fashioned bathtub. I moved towards it and opened the door wider. I entered a strange reality; or, now as I think about it, a heightened reality. My eyes felt more powerful, as though I gazed at the images before me through a microscope.

I could see the pores of the vicar's face. Each hair on his head was in focus. I could read the words *James Walker and Sons, Sheffield, England* on the concave, polished blade of the straight razor in his hand. His black shirt, minus his white clerical collar, was hanging forward, exposing part of his chest; his white elastic braces were pushed down off his shoulders. On the creased skin of his throat in the blood which had run down his neck was a bluebottle. I could see the veins in its wings and its back legs twitching and rubbing together. The vicar lay on the floor. He was dead.

I'd never seen a dead body before. I could hear a chaffinch chirping outside the open window as though nothing was wrong. A second bluebottle buzzed madly around my head. Then it alighted on Dr Snipe's upper lip and jumped a half turn. I

watched the obscene rubbing of its back legs as it
tasted the object it had landed upon. I stood still.
The tap dripped into the washbasin of water. I saw a
swirl of blood. Thunder rumbled above, then
cracked. It seemed much, much longer, but could
have been only a few seconds before I screamed
Blum's name. I stepped back from the body and
fled, collided with an arriving Blum.

'What's up?'

I couldn't speak, but he looked past me and saw
Dr Snipe sprawled on the floor where he died. He
stepped forward and regarded the body for a few
moments. I found my voice, 'We've got to tell Mrs.
Beattie. We've got to go now!'

Blum stepped over the body and reached up to
the open transom of the window. He jiggled the
catch, pulled it shut.

Dumbfounded at his casual attitude, I said, 'What
are you doing?'

Blum swatted the bluebottles away from Dr
Snipe's face. He was matter of fact, 'Anymore of
'em get in he'll be blummin' maggotted.'

He seemed so casual about the dead body on the
floor. I wondered if it had anything to do with his
father's death not long before. Blum told me, almost
with pride, that he'd seen his dad as a corpse.

He steered me out and shut the inner door.
Thunder cracked again. We ran.

*

NOW, ON TOP of the gravestone, I thought about
finding Dr Snipe dead. Was his soul here with us as
we watched the three men still in whispered

conversation? Was he angry with us for what we planned, that went against those commandments we had heard him speak of so many times in the Big Room at school? I had an alarming image of him summoning others in the graveyard like Ellen Sossin and pointing at us with a ghostly finger, revealing our intentions to the restless souls.

My thoughts were interrupted by the movement of the men. While the first man looked about, the other two strode towards the front door of the vicarage. I thought they were going to knock, but they veered away, went round to the back, retracing our own steps that afternoon. The first man hurried after them and we looked at each other. Blum was frustrated. 'What the 'eck are they doing?'

'Let's leave it and go, eh?'

'We've got blummin' ages before we have to get home.'

A light came on in the vicarage. It shone through the glass panel above the front door.

Blum slithered down from the top of the gravestone, 'I'm going to look at them cars.'

Before I could say anything, he was away. He swung himself over the lower front wall of the churchyard, went out of sight behind the big elder tree. I turned back to the light shining across the un-cut grass of the vicarage's front lawn.

Thunder and lightning crossed a dark sky as Blum and me fled over that same grass earlier in the day; ran as fast as we could to tell Mrs. Beattie the vicar was dead. I had a stitch in my side and Blum grazed a knee as he tripped on a kerbstone, but we had to keep going. We passed some of our own classmates on their way home, but ignored their shouted questions about our haste as they plodded through the rain. We clattered, soaked, into the Big Room as Mrs. Beattie watered the geraniums on the window ledges and Hetty Hothersall put on her cycle gloves and brown beret. Mrs. Beattie's expression radiated anger at our lateness, but turned to disquiet in moments as we gasped out the details of our discovery at the vicarage.

In between her repeated remarks -- 'Poor Dr Snipe,' 'How terrible for you boys' -- Hetty sat us down and brought us beakers of water while Mrs. Beattie hurried to the school house for towels to dry us and to telephone the police. She returned and took us to the school house. We sat in the parlour, a room we'd been within yards of for almost seven years without ever seeing. There she lit a fire and urged us to drink cups of sickly sweet tea while she went to another room to telephone people we told her could pass messages to our mothers.

Mrs. Beattie had other telephone calls to make, it seemed, and we were left alone. I stared at a framed print of *The Laughing Cavalier*, reliving my discovery of Dr Snipe's body when Blum interrupted me, to reveal his startling plan for us to return to the vicarage that night – to take the Hardy fishing rod.

I was shocked. 'We can't.'

'We can if we want,' said Blum.

'It's …It's stealing from a dead man.'

'Ha. You've heard old Snipey yourself. "We come into this world with nowt and we go out with nowt." Even mam says it often enough. How can it be stealing if he's dead?'

He suggested the late carp fishing expedition to disguise our return to the vicarage, predicted our mothers would be soft on us after the experience of finding a dead man while running an errand for our headmistress. I liked the idea of going out late, but not his intention to take the rod. I shook my head.

'But you could get that old book.'

I was appalled, 'No.'

Blum shrugged,' Why not? Snipey won't be reading it again, will he?'

I hesitated a moment, felt the pull of temptation. Then shook my head.

'If you don't want it, fair play,' said Blum. He added, 'I could do with a look-out, mind'

'All right,' I said, 'But I'm not going back inside.'

Blum nodded as we heard Mrs. Beattie open her front door and the anxious voices of our mothers.

*

MY EYES WERE fixed on the panel of light above the front door of the vicarage. I failed to hear Blum's return and was startled as I heard the scrabble of shoe leather behind me and Blum re-joined me on top of Ellen Sossin's headstone.

He whispered, 'That other car -- It's a blummin' hearse.'

'What? You mean one of them funeral things?'

'A coffin wagon, yeah, they must be the undertakers come to fetch old Snipey.'

I felt a sense of relief the body was about to be taken away, but it was replaced by the fear Blum might now expect me to join him inside the vicarage.

We heard the scrape of a stiff bolt and then light flooded from the open front door. We peered over the wall. A man backed out of the door carrying one end of a long object. The man carrying the other end came into view as they moved on to the path. The front man spoke in a low voice. They stopped while the front man turned to face forward. They started to walk faster towards the road.

Blum whispered, 'There goes old Snipey, tucked up in his box.'

'That's not a coffin,' my voice was a gasp. Blum clapped his hand across my mouth. I pulled it away and whispered, 'It's the vicar's grandfather clock -- that big one in the hall.'

Blum raised himself higher, using the cover of some holly branches, to get a better view. At that moment, the man who arrived in the Zephyr, came out of the vicarage. In his arms was a big oil painting of a sailing ship in a harbour. I remembered glimpsing it on the stairs. The thick, gilt frame shone in the light. It confirmed our sudden suspicion.

'They're robbing the vicarage!' said Blum.

We watched as the grandfather clock and the picture were stowed in the back of the Zephyr. The driver lit a cigarette. 'I'll get this lot tucked up out the way. Back in half an hour,' he said.

'Make sure you are,' said one of the others.

'Stay out the Golden Lion an' all,' said the third. The driver laughed, went to the Zephyr.

One man went to move the hearse closer to the drive. The other went back in the house and was joined a minute later by his fellow thief. We watched as they brought out items of furniture, pictures and silverware and piled them into the back of the hearse, covering them with blankets. Other items which wouldn't fit in the vehicle were piled up on the grass.

'Shouldn't we go and call the police?' I said.

'Nah, not yet,' said Blum, 'Let's wait 'til that other feller gets back, so they all get nabbed.'

We carried on with our watch and the Zephyr returned. As soon as they started to carry their loot from the grass to the second vehicle, Blum said, 'Now's the time. I'll go and ring from the phone box on the main road.'

I made a move to join him, but he said, 'I thought you were lookout? If they drive off you'll have to run and tell me what way they go, so's I can tell the police.'

'I can go and ring nine, nine, nine,' I said.

'Don't be daft. You'll never remember the car numbers.'

'What car numbers?'

Blum tapped his head, 'The ones I've had in here since I went to have a gander.'

He slipped down off the gravestone, 'Watch everything and remember it,' he whispered, then disappeared into the darkness of the graveyard.

Blum was back in five minutes with a grin on his face and pleased to see the thieves still at work. It seemed no time at all before we saw blue lights and then heard the siren. We stayed at our established vantage point as three police cars and a bobby on a Velocette motor bike came up the lane at speed. The two men who were loading the hearse seemed mesmerised at the sound and light, but the Zephyr driver snatched the fag from his mouth and rushed down the drive to his car. It didn't seem to occur to him that he couldn't turn around and the lane was blocked by police cars, out of which now piled seven bobbies. The Zephyr driver was in an arm lock before he could get his ignition key out of his overall pocket. Outnumbered by uniforms, the other two were each manhandled into the back of two separate panda cars.

The scene was surveyed by a sergeant with a ginger moustache and two constables, who wandered on to the vicarage driveway to look at the vicar's property lying on the grass.

Blum slipped down from Ellen Sossin's gravestone. He picked up his rod and tackle from the foot of the wall. 'Better show our faces, then.'

To my horror, Blum was about to announce our presence to the sergeant. I thought we'd slip away when we had the chance. I was in a sweat. What if they questioned us about our presence in the churchyard after dark?

'What about…You know?' I whispered.

He grinned at me, 'That old book, you fancy?'

'You know what I mean, the Roach Perfection?'

Blum laughed and turned away. I needn't have worried about the planned burglary slipping out in the presence of authority. While the constables carted the thieves' booty back into the vicarage, I nodded and chipped in as required when Blum described to Sergeant Bickerstaffe our suspicions at seeing furniture being taken out of the vicarage on our way home from a late fishing session; that we knew the vicar had died that day because we'd found him.

The Sergeant thanked us and warned us we'd have to make statements over the next few days.

'Just give me two ticks and I'll run you both home and speak to your mothers,' he said. He turned back to the matter in hand and called to the youngest bobby, 'Hang on a minute, Drewery.'

The young copper picked up a silver coffee pot, 'Yes, Sarge.'

'The CID'll want to have a look round, so you'd better stay on 'til the morning and keep your eyes open. I don't want anyone in or out of that vicarage 'til the jacks've seen what's what.'

Drewery couldn't hide his reluctance, 'Me, Sarge?'

'Yes, you,' confirmed his superior. Drewery's face had gone white.

Blum butted in, 'No need to worry about anyone going in and out. The vicar was found dead this afternoon.'

Drewery threw a nervous glance back at the vicarage, 'Where?'

'In there,' Blum said, pointing to the vicarage, 'Where do you think?'

*

THE NEXT TWO weeks passed in a blur of excitement and notoriety. Mrs. Beattie and Hetty Hothersall fussed over us when we returned to school on Monday. Our classmates were hungry for details of Dr Snipe's death. We made statements about the thieves to Sergeant Bickerstaffe over the weekend and a few days later gave more statements to Constable Drewery about finding the vicar dead.

Both of us were nervous when we attended the inquest in Ormskirk, but our statements were read out to the court. The pathologist reported that the vicar had died of a heart attack while shaving; not an unusual occurrence when someone is eighty-two. It was a relief as rumours had it Dr Snipe had 'topped' himself. The Coroner recorded a death from natural causes. No doubt some in the parish had twinges of guilt that they'd pushed for the old man's removal.

We were still worried about giving evidence against the burglars, but our parents were told the thieves had been caught in the act and were sensible enough to admit everything. Two of the men were the undertakers' assistants who collected Dr Snipe's body at the request of the police and coroner late on the afternoon of his death. Their plan involved bringing in the third man to making a quick killing by selling Dr Snipe's possessions to a crooked antique dealer in Southport.

At school we were feted for having our names in the Thursday *Advertiser* two weeks on the trot. Once in the vicar's inquest report on Page 5, then again under a photograph of Blum and me on the front page; me holding a landing net and Blum a rod with the headline, 'Young anglers help police net vicarage thieves.' I felt awkward and embarrassed about the publicity, but Blum enjoyed it.

The last day of summer term arrived and, for the first time in living memory, the end- of- term book prizes were not presented by Dr Snipe. Instead, some big-wig none of us had heard of stood in for him. I contained my slight disappointment that no prize was forthcoming for me, even though I'd worked hard on two compositions on subjects I didn't find dull.

Blum and I walked home on the last afternoon before the holidays. We stopped off to watch kingfishers diving for roach fry and jack sharps at Billy's Bridge. We sat on the sandstone parapet dangling our legs over the cut, talking of things we might do in the holidays, but I could tell Blum had something on his mind as we left the kingfishers and headed home along the towpath.

His silence lasted for a hundred yards before he said, 'You didn't get a prize then?'

I looked at him. Was he joking? But there was no sign of humour in his return glance.

'Loads of us liked what you wrote about the nature stuff you see on the cut and the other one about harvest time.' He paused a moment, 'I thought they were blummin' good and all.'

I was a touch embarrassed at a mate's praise for something I didn't talk about much. We continued along the towpath in silence. Part of me had hoped for some recognition for at least one of the two pieces of work which we had to read out in front the whole school. Another part of me, though, hated the idea of being associated with regular prize winners like Gillian Sumner and one or two others.

Blum's voice snapped me back from my thoughts.

'Don't be too fed up, mind,' he said. He stopped, pulled his school satchel off his shoulder and held it to his chest. His hand burrowed under the flap and pulled out a book. He held it up to me, 'I've been saving this old thing for yer.'

My mouth dropped open. It was the copy of *Three Men in a Boat* signed by Jerome K. Jerome for Dr Snipe.

Blum grinned at me like the village idiot. 'I thought you might change your mind about having it now everything's died down and that…'

He held it out to me and I took it.

'It's still got that old postcard inside an' all,' he said.

I stared at the book. Then looked at Blum. He now seemed uncertain, 'How did you get it?'

Blum paused for a moment, rubbed the back of his neck.

'I had to have that rod…'

'You've got that as well?'

He nodded.

'How?'

Blum looked around, as if there might be an eavesdropper, 'Remember that Sergeant Bickerstaffe dropping us off the night old Snipey pegged it? Well, when he'd had a talk to me mam, I said I was tired and went to bed, but I didn't. I sneaked me bike out and went back up along the cut. Left it at Pilling Bridge and went across Cyril Clegg's land 'til I was opposite the vicarage...'

'What about that copper who had to stay all night?'

Blum grinned, 'I knew he was frittened as soon as Sergeant Bickerstaffe said he had to guard the place. That's why I said about Snipey being found dead -- to put the wind up him, like. All it took were a bit of owl calling and a few clods lobbed in the bushes behind him and he was off down to the main road to stand under the lamp post by the phone box.' Blum chuckled, his eyes twinkled, 'I was in and out that old junk shop in two minutes.'

I had to laugh, but I was unsure about the book, 'I don't think I should keep it.'

'It's not stealing.'

'It feels like it to me.'

Blum sighed, 'I knew you'd say that, but I thought about it. What them fellers did, that was stealing. They didn't care about the things they took off an old man who was dead. They weren't going to keep them and look after them, were they? They didn't even know him like we did. They were just going to flog 'em to get money.'

He paused. I looked at the book again.

Blum continued, 'I know you'll look after it and every time you read it you'll think about old Snipey. I'll do the same with that rod. Every fish I catch with it…it'll be like he's with me catching it and I'll be thinking of him and the fish he caught with it, like them Tiggy salmon and chub things in that photo.'

I opened the book and read the inscription, then pulled out the card and read Jerome's postcard to his young reader.

Blum waited. After a while, he said, 'Do you want to keep it?'

I remembered the picture of Dr Snipe with JKJ. I nodded.

Blum beamed, 'Ha, we both got prizes from the vicar, then.'

*

OVER THE YEARS I have re-read that book many times. It turned out to be an 1889 first edition and worth a considerable sum, but I would never sell it. The postcard is now in a frame alongside two photographs; one of Dr Snipe with the Tigris salmon and mangar fish (like Blum guessed, one of the carp family, which includes the chub) and the other of our former vicar with Jerome K. Jerome. My mother thought I'd gone daft when I heard some of the vicar's bric-a-brac was being put in a jumble sale to help church funds and paid half a crown for both pictures; I also took the opportunity to ease my conscience over the book and told her it was included with the photos. I regretted I didn't buy one of those pictures of him with his beautiful wife, Dora.

For later in life when I worked as a journalist I looked into the life of Dr Snipe and his early career as an archaeologist in modern-day Syria, Turkey and Iraq. I wrote a feature article, minus any mention of my presence on the day of his death. During the early years of their marriage, Dora wrote dozens of articles for the New York and London magazines about their travels and work in the Middle East. Crispin Snipe had written an important work about early civilisation to earn his doctorate at Oxford and could read and write Hebrew, Aramaic and classical Greek.

Dora was an early travel writer, the daughter of a wealthy Scottish family. Dr Snipe married her after they met at a mutual friend's home in Alexandria. In only a few years, she spent much of a substantial inheritance putting promising students from Mesopotamia through medical school and establishing schools in remote communities. She always accompanied her new husband on archaeological digs, both helping him and attending, unofficially, to the medical needs of the dig labourers and local people.

Months before the First World War, Dora died of typhus while on a dig near the Euphrates River. From my research into the correspondence and memoirs of friends and contemporaries of Dr Snipe, I discovered he was so distraught at the loss of his wife, he returned to England and joined the waves of volunteers for service in Flanders. Despite his background and scholarship, he declined a commission and served as a private. He survived the carnage of Passchendaele, the Somme and other campaigns and sickened at the futility of war, became a pacifist and followed a calling as a clergyman in London, Burnley, Leyland and Lydiate.

It saddened me that he lost his beautiful, young wife in such circumstances. I was also sorry that a man who had given so much to the study and understanding of ancient civilisation had reached the fringes of senility and had been reviled for it in some parts of our village. He didn't deserve such a mundane and lonely death.

Years later, Blum's mam passed on to me some of his personal possessions. Among them was the Reverend Dr. Crispin Snipe's Hardy split-cane fishing rod. I can't say it brought me luck. I used it twice for old times' sake, but caught nothing. But I can never touch the old varnish and maroon silk whippings without an image coming to mind. It is from a frosty Sunday morning on a Plough Horse fishing club trip to the River Dee at Chester. Blum and I were teenagers. It is a treasured moment of our friendship.

Winter sun slants across grey, sliding water. Blum stands on a plank jetty and grins to himself as he casts a maggot and trots it downstream. His float travels perhaps twenty feet. Blum's hand twitches the Hardy Roach Perfection in a delicate strike. The split-cane arcs as a patrolling chub is hooked. The sun catches its twisting silver flank as it fights the tightened line; the varnished bamboo flashes, a bolt of golden lightning. Blum turns to me. We each know the other's thoughts. He smiles and his eyes shine as a dead man lives again, if only for an instant.

Mustard Lugs and the Toads

WE STARED IN disbelief as the yellow earth shifter's massive bucket scraped up a heap of sandy soil and swung to dump it by the water's edge.

Only last weekend we'd mooched round the old asparagus farm and it was in the same dilapidated, yet tranquil, state as it had been since we were five-year-olds. Now, peace and quiet had given way to chaos and the roar of a powerful diesel engine.

Builders had dug footings for a dozen semi-detached houses. Mixer lorries had poured tons of concrete into the trenches and already the first brick courses of one house had been laid. The nearest set of footings was only forty yards from the two shallow ponds which filled with water over winter and dried up by mid-summer.

Nearly all the long, raised beds, that once provided bundles of 'sparagus' for West End hotels had been destroyed. Within five days, while we were at school and unaware, one of our favourite places had been spoilt forever.

In those days many fields, where once we shot rats along the ditches, fished the pits for perch and rudd and spent our holidays picking peas, broad beans and spuds, had been turned into private housing estates for newcomers. People had to live somewhere, but this was vandalism, sacrilege; a disaster. This piece of land wasn't any old field -- it was a sanctuary for a rare toad, the natter jack.

The earth shifter emptied, then clanked back into place, Blum and me swapped a look. We were shocked. 'What about the toads?' I said.

Blum was seething with suppressed anger, 'They can't do this, it's not right.'

The roaring earth shifter reversed away from the ponds and turned towards the entrance of the smallholding which had now become a building site. The deafening engine noise cut out and the driver jumped down and went towards the site hut.

As peace returned, we heard the croaking of the toads. 'They've started,' said Blum.

We pushed through a gap in the old hawthorn hedge alongside the canal towpath, down a steep bank and hurried toward the ponds. As we moved closer we could see the shallows of the first pond alive with natter jacks, jostling and crawling over each other, as they prepared to mate and spawn. Their croaks sounded like those of frogs, but more urgent, louder.

We skirted the first pond and approached the second. Each was only the size of a tennis court, but for years, they were the only place in the parish where natter jack toads bred.

In the second pond, we found a similar breeding frenzy. Dozens more natter jacks ignored us as they searched for mates, the males croaking on top note; the single yellow line down each of their backs highlighted in the spring sunlight.

'Do you reckon they'll build over the pond, or fill it in, or something?' I said.

Blum was squatting at the water's edge, his eyes on the toads, 'I don't know, but there should be a law against this.'

We heard a shout, 'Oi! You!'

A big man in overalls and a donkey jacket came away from some huge blocks of building brick, each block bound and packed in plastic sheeting. He strode towards us, continuing to shout, 'Bugger off out of it. This is private land.'

'Quick! Leg it!' said Blum and we turned and sprinted round the ponds, back up the bank to the canal.

Blum pushed through the hedge at the top with me right behind him. Even as we legged away, I was puzzled. It wasn't like Blum to give ground. I could think of half a dozen times when we'd been accosted for trespass and he refused to leave without forcing the challenger to threaten either the law, or physical violence. At the very least he would act daft, or make sarcastic remarks. This wasn't his way.

We walked along the cinder towpath of the canal, looked back. Donkey Jacket had given up the chase before he even reached the ponds, but he was still shouting.

'Keep out of it. If see you on here again, I'll get the bloody police on yer.'

I would've expected Blum to shout back an insult. Or perhaps stick up two fingers. Instead, he pushed me in the back and loped away along the towpath. I glanced back at Donkey Jacket, but he was already on his way to the site hut.

We reached the clump of sycamore at the end of the asparagus farm, out of the sight of the builders. Blum stopped and peered through the trees. I joined him. Donkey Jacket was talking to two other men. One leaned a brick hod against the earth shifter; another wiped a brickie's trowel with a piece of concrete sack. Donkey Jacket rolled a fag.

'Why did we leg it?' I said.

'I don't want him recognising me again.'

'Shouldn't we tell him about the toads, tell him they're spawning?'

Blum's eyes remained on the distant figures, 'Nah, he's the sort who'd drive that bulldozer thing through the ponds just to spite us.'

'You don't know that. We could've explained -- '

Blum cut me off, faced me, 'He's a destroyer.'

This was his term for anyone who tried to change the face of our parish in even the smallest way. In his head it included anyone who felled a mature tree, a farmer who pulled out a hedge to enlarge a field or filled in a fishing pond with chat spuds and other rubbish. In the main, it was now his description for the builders of new houses, which had begun to transform our mostly rural surroundings.

'He's just a feller who's…'

'He's a destroyer who doesn't care what he does as long as there's money in it. We should get him for this.'

'Doing his job, you mean?'

'Ha, his job's not worth a carrot.'

'Don't be soft.'

But Blum was serious, 'Them natter jacks have been there for years, ten thousand blummin' years for all we know. What gives someone the right to just build over their territory, eh?'

He jabbed a finger towards the new houses, 'That feller couldn't care less as long as he gets his wages. Just like whoever owns Burstyn's now. They make money and bugger the toads.'

Ronnie Burstyn had been the final owner of the twelve or-so-acre asparagus farm. His wife died young and their short marriage, minus any children, marked the end of a family line that had grown asparagus since the coming of the railways enabled them to send their crop as far as London within a day. Ronnie was now dead and ownership of the sandy piece of one-time heath, perfect ground to grow asparagus, was reputed to have passed years ago to a distant relative in Canada. Now, it seemed, they'd sold it to building developers.

Blum snatched a sycamore switch and stripped the leaves off it with a stroke of his hand. He slashed it against the trunk of the nearest tree.

'What was that about him recognising you?' I said, 'You don't know him do you?'

He shook his head, 'Nah. I wouldn't want to either.'

'Why bother about it, then?'

He grinned at me, 'I don't want him knowing owt about me, bugger-all, 'cause I'm going to stop him.'

I was scornful. 'You can't stop a building site.'

'I might be able to stop it 'til the spawning's over and done. And muck him up a bit while I'm about it.' He pondered for a moment, swishing the switch. Then looked at me, 'Did you hear 'em last night?'

In spring times past, I'd often heard the natter jacks croaking at night, even though I lived three hundred yards away. Their voices would carry clearly on a windless night like last night, but I'd heard nothing. 'No, not a croak.'

'Right,' said Blum. He launched the switch into the cut like a spear. 'It takes them three days to mate and spawn and they've just started. So we don't want them disturbed 'til at least Tuesday.'

He turned back to look at Burstyn's. 'Them builders are knocking off now and they shouldn't be back 'til Monday morning. We've got a bit of time to sort summat out. Fancy a walk to the chippy while I have a think?'

*

IN THE ABSENCE of Donkey Jacket and his men, we ate our chips, sitting cross-legged, while we watched the natter jacks continue their annual courtship and mating.

Later, the shallows of the ponds would be full of spawn; single black eggs nestled inside transparent jelly ribbons at regular intervals along its length and reminiscent of the tapes of banger caps we once used in toy pistols. More ribbons of spawn would appear on Sunday and Monday before the adult toads dispersed by Tuesday, leaving the eggs to their fate.

'What about after? When the taddies hatch?' I said.

Blum shrugged. 'Better pray for a load of warm weather to speed things up.'

We knew that natter jack tadpoles turned into fully-formed toadlets faster than common toads and frogs. As they lived and bred only in dry, sandy places with seasonal ponds, nature had accelerated the process so the young ones were on their way before the breeding ponds dried up.

We finished our chips and mooched across to dump the papers in the builders' oil drum brazier. Blum picked up a piece of 2x2 wood and poked them down until the embers set the paper alight.

'One day the whole soddin' place'll be covered in bricks and concrete,' he said. He kicked the drum and sparks flared up in the smoke. He looked at me, 'I'm not just talking about here. I mean everywhere. Then what happens? What do birds and animals -- even the insects and flowers -- what do they do then?'

I'd never considered such a future. But I was concerned about this year's natter jacks. Even if they survived, where would they live? People would start new lives here soon, but for the natter jacks the back gardens of modern houses without suitable water for breeding meant no future for them.

When we were younger we would catch the toadlets, though we soon realised we couldn't keep them in captivity. Without a constant supply of food insects it was hopeless; they always died. Instead, we learned to observe them. From fresh hatched taddies to brand new baby toads, Blum and me would act as their guardians and scare off any younger kids we caught equipped with jam jars and intent on repeating our misguided attempts to raise them away from their source of food.

I watched Blum as he moved away, swinging the piece of wood and slapping it against his wellie boot. He seemed in a low mood as he stood and stared at the mass of building bricks. He poked at the plastic wrapping with the wood. After a while, he moved towards the entrance of the smallholding. It was a narrow track on to Silver Birches lane. On one side was the Burstyns' tumbledown house, which had boards nailed over its doors and windows. On the other was a tall hedge, behind which lay two other semi-detached workmen's cottages, one owned by an old woman, the other to a man known to all as Mustard Lugs.

I never knew why he was called Mustard Lugs. Before he retired, he was the roadman who pushed his barrow up and down the lanes cleaning gutters, making smaller repairs and talking rubbish, mostly to himself. He was a strong and stocky man who was once in the Navy. He must have acquired the habit on board ship for he was never without a flask of rum in his pocket. More than once, before and after his retirement as roadman, we had found him snoring drunk at the roadside, well before the sun was over the yardarm. On one occasion we took advantage of his unconsciousness to take a close look at his ears, but there was no indication why he acquired such an odd nickname. His most obvious physical feature was his ginger hair, flecked with only a trace of grey.

I wandered over to Blum as he became animated. He hurried to the back of Burstyn's cottage and with the piece of wood, started to scrape a line in the dirt and cinder ground. He moved backwards, dragging the stick in the dirt until he reached almost the back of Mustard Lugs' place. He then repeated the action, scraping another line parallel to the first, but some four feet from the original. Each line was about fifteen yards long.

'Have you gone doolally?' I said.

'I know what to do,' said a triumphant Blum. He started to scrape another line.

'What?'

But Blum was too busy to reply. He concentrated on the job as he drew five parallel lines. From the first line to the fifth was about twenty feet. He finished the scraping and regarded the lines with satisfaction. He threw the piece of wood aside, 'Let's get crackin'. I reckon we've got 'til about half-seven Monday morning.'

*

WE WORKED LIKE navvies. It was worse for our hands than cutting sprouts in the frost, as back-breaking as picking spuds. Work started straight away that Saturday afternoon and we kept going without stopping until we had to go home for tea. I thought we could take the evening off, but Blum declared we needed to come back and work, even when it went dark.

By the time it came to half-past nine, we both had to keep to our parents' curfew. Even if we hadn't, we'd both had enough of the labour. We'd worked in turn, one carrying bricks from the massive pile, the other building. It was easier and faster than if we had to mortar the bricks together, but the work was still gruelling. My hands were numb and I had a blister on one finger. My arms felt like they'd been pulled from their sockets.

Blum examined his hands by the light of a little battery torch, 'We need gloves for tomorrow.'

'We're doing this again?' The thought horrified me. 'Isn't this enough?'

'Nowhere near,' Blum said. 'I marked-up five lines, we need five walls.' He shone the torch on what we'd achieved.

We'd built two, parallel fifteen-yard walls right across the entrance to the asparagus farm. By trial and error, we'd created a design of interlocked bricks, positioning them with gaps between, but making a solid structure which could not be pushed down, at least not by any human being. Each wall was about five feet high and three-feet thick.

'This'll take hours to take down,' I said.

'We don't want it to take hours; we want it to take all day, two days'd be better,' said Blum. 'I want to use every blummin' brick they've got.'

I pointed to the earth shifter, 'What if they use that and just push it all out of the way?'

'How many bricks'd get smashed if they did that? How much money would that cost? What do you think Donkey Jacket's boss is going to say if he tells them they've got to buy more bricks?'

He laughed. 'There's nowt they can do about it, only take this down by hand and carry the bricks back where they came from.'

*

AT SIX 'O CLOCK on the Sunday morning we met up at Burstyn's. I could hear the natter jacks croaking from the minute I slipped out of our back door. As planned, we brought sandwiches and a drink and both of us now had gloves. Despite this luxury, our hands were still sore. I felt like my back would never allow me to bend over ever again, but we had work to do.

By the time the church bell started to chime, we'd started the fourth wall. To speed up the job we tried to use the brickie's hod to carry a bigger number of bricks. It was a failure. Hods were not designed to be carried by skinny lads, so we went back to carrying one brick in each hand. We both had to be back for Sunday dinner, but returned early afternoon to finish the fourth wall. We'd told our mothers we'd be having tea at each other's houses, so we were able to carry on. By evening, the fifth wall was complete. We'd created a barrier twenty yards long, about nine yards wide and five feet high.

I felt a great sense of achievement, but Blum was troubled by the remaining stacks of bricks. He stood tapping his head, brooding and thinking.

'I know what to do with them' I said, pointed, 'Build another wall round that.'

Blum grinned, 'You're a blummin' genius. Come on, before it goes dark.'

With our knitted gloves in tatters and our muscles aching, we managed to finish as the lights over on the main road started to come on. Blum stood on tiptoes to push the last two bricks into position and we stepped back to admire the finishing touch to the weekend's work. I fancied the toads' frenzied croaking was like an appreciative audience as we stepped back to admire the earth shifter imprisoned inside a thick six-foot high wall.

We'd love to have been outside the asparagus farm when Donkey Jacket and his men arrived early on Monday, but we knew it was too risky. And like many practical jokes, the pleasure is often better left to the imagination -- or hearing of the result through the accounts of eye-witnesses.

*

ON MONDAY EVENING we didn't have the benefit of any witnesses, but as we sauntered along Silver Birches lane to the entrance of Burstyn's we were pleased to see the builders had not had a productive day's house-building. The toads were still croaking, but the volume was lower and less constant. About half our walls were dismantled. It looked like Donkey Jacket had split his team for one of the new house walls was slightly higher, while the rescued bricks were stacked back in their original position.

'Look,' said Blum. I followed his finger. The earth shifter was as we left it, still captive in its brick fold, like a mechanical beast. I laughed as I looked at it, imagined the outrage Donkey Jacket must have felt that morning.

Blum whooped in delight. I looked to see him gloating over a huge pile of broken bricks which had been dumped to one side.

'Ha, serves them blummin' right,' he said. He chuckled, 'I bet that's cost 'em more than a few bob, eh?'

The thought that we'd caused financial damage made me a touch uneasy. 'Let's go and check the toads,' I said.

The mating was almost over. Most of the adult toads had gone. Both ponds were full of spawn ribbons. We stooped down for a better look

'Looks like the wall did the trick,' said Blum.

'For how long, though?'

I heard a shout.

Blum stood, 'Who's this?'

A figure made its way across from our still-standing walls.

I laughed, 'It's only Mustard Lugs.'

He swayed as he crossed a wrecked asparagus bed.

'Looks like he's blummin' kaylied to me.'

Mustard Lugs lumbered towards us, 'What you doing on here? This is private.'

'Just out for a bit of a walk,' said Blum.

Mustard pointed to the entrance, 'Back the way you come -- now.'

'We're not doing any harm,' said Blum, 'We've been coming through here for ages, always have.'

'Aye, well not no more, it's private now,' Mustard nodded back towards the entrance, 'Building new 'ouses, see.'

'Doesn't mean we can't walk through' said Blum.

'I'm telling you, you can't.'

Blum was defiant, 'You can't stop us.'

Mustard narrowed his watery grey eyes, 'I can now. I'm new night watchman.'

Blum laughed. 'You?'

'Aye, as from today, so sling your hook, the pair of yer. I only have to knock at Mrs. Silcock's and she'll ring up police.'

Blum laughed, 'Oh, aye?'

'Don't cheek me, son. Boss on here's told me I can call police anytime anyone sets foot.'

'Then best tell Mrs. Silcock it's Whitehall one, two, one two.'

Mustard frowned, 'Eh?'

Blum laughed, 'It's the phone number at Scotland Yard.'

We turned away and headed towards the entrance.

'Afore you go…'

We looked back.

Mustard Lugs cocked his head to one side and stared at us, 'Were you on here over weekend?'

'Us? Nah. Why?' said Blum.

Again, Mustard's watery eyes squinted as he observed our faces.

'Never you mind,' he said, 'Just keep off!'

*

BLUM WAS MUCH amused by the appointment of Mustard Lugs as night watchman. 'How can he be a cocky watchman when he's drunk before dinnertime? Mrs. Silcock told mam he drinks rum before he has his porridge. Wonder if them blummin' builders know that?'

But Mustard's new appointment made it difficult to check when the tadpoles hatched and how soon they might be ready to leave the water. I suggested we could use Blum's grandfather's field glasses and check the ponds from the canal bank. A day or two later we arrived with the field glasses and took up a position under an elder bush on the towpath overlooking the building site.

The tadpoles were hatching in their hundreds. Not many of them would become toadlets, though, for their enemies were legion and we could do nothing to protect the weakest from magpies, crows, frogs, dragonfly larvae and water boatmen; even the cannibal tendencies of their own stronger brothers and sisters.

I swore as a lone carrion crow hopped through the pond shallows, cherry-picking fat taddies. Blum chuckled.

'It's not funny. I hate bloody crows,' I said.

'I don't mean the blummin' crow.' he said, 'Give us the glasses.'

I handed them over, 'What is it?'

'It's Mustard.' He snorted a laugh as he focused across the field, 'Look at him. He's landed the blummin' plum job all right.'

Blum passed back the glasses and I looked across the field.

'Just this side of his own back garden. Look at him. Snug as the bug in the rug.'

I moved the field glasses in that direction and saw the reason for Blum's merriment.

The builders had provided their new watchman with a headquarters. It was a small garden shed.

Inside, with the door wide open, Mustard reclined in an old armchair with a flask of rum in his hand. Beside him was a table with a paraffin lantern, a Primus stove, kettle, teapot and all the bits and pieces to brew up. From his position he could see the new houses as well as the ponds. He swigged some Captain Morgan, adjusted his position to get more comfortable. Mustard Lugs was at peace with the world on this late April evening.

Blum took back the glasses and had another look at the idle watchman.

'Do you reckon he stays there all night,' I said.

'Well he is tonight.'

'Eh?'

Blum was already moving. 'Come on.'

We went down the canal and turned off at the next bridge. In a few minutes we were on Silver Birches lane, approaching the entrance to Burstyn's. Donkey Jacket had installed a makeshift barrier of wire netting across the entrance, but we crawled through the narrow gap at one end, where it was tied into the hedge with wire.

We moved round the corner of the old lady's garden. We could see Mustard's new shed side on. Blum put his finger to his lips and we crept round the pile of broken bricks to within a few feet of the shed. Blum pointed to the tiny window in the side of the shed and then to his eye. I understood and followed him forward.

We heard Mustard Lugs' slurred command, 'Halt! Who goes there?'

We froze. Had he detected our approach? How?

The voice continued, 'Easy, me old jack tar. I'm shipping some rum, but I'll be away to me bunk afore you can say Admiral Lord Nelson an' raise a glass, God bless him.'

I sniggered. It sounded like Mustard was having a conversation with himself. Blum grinned as he put his finger to his temple and rotated his finger back and forth; he's barmy. Mustard Lugs continued rambling. We moved to the shed, stooping low, and then raised our heads to peer through the side window. Mustard drained his flask of rum and slapped it down on the table. He gave a loud, rumble of a belch and settled back.

Blum moved to the front of the shed and quick as a flash slammed the door shut. He shot the bolt and we looked in the window. We expected an outraged Mustard Lugs, but he was slumped in his chair fast asleep.

Laughing, we went to the ponds to check the tadpoles. Despite their exposure to crows and other predators, the ponds still teemed. We left Mustard Lugs to be freed next morning by Donkey Jacket and his men.

*

WE KEPT A covert watch on the tadpoles over following days using the field glasses. All that time they were undisturbed by the building activity. Then disaster came. I was biking back from school along the canal towpath. I saw the movement of the earth shifter from a hundred yards away, its neck and bucket rearing up above the elder tree we used as an observation point.

When I stopped at the elder, I was shocked. Strings and pegs had been measured out across the ends of the two ponds. Already, water was draining from the ponds into a new footings trench. Two men with a diesel pump were pumping out the trench and gouts of water spewed out of the pipe at the back of the pump to run across the field towards the entrance to the farm . Each second that passed meant tadpoles were being pumped to their deaths in a dry wasteland of churned earth and concrete dust.

I watched, shocked for a moment, and then pedalled off as fast as I could. I found Blum getting off the bus from his school near the driveway of May Bank View. In my upset I garbled out what I'd seen. Blum was incensed as he let out a string of random swear words, but I knew he was thinking fast.

He led the way up the drive to the outbuildings behind his house. Ten minutes later, we left on our bikes with all the things Blum reckoned we needed packed in a wet hessian potato sack over his handlebars

We chucked our bikes into the long grass on the canal bank and Blum hefted the dripping sack. We were about to push through the hedge when we saw Mustard Lugs swaying as he walked from the new buildings to his shed. In our panic to put our plan into action we'd forgotten about Mustard's new job. We ducked out of sight and watched him through the hedge. He paused and pulled a flask from his pocket. He unscrewed the top and, tilting back his head, tipped rum down his throat.

We waited, wondering what he would do next. Mustard replaced his flask and looked around him. Then walked back to his shed, opened the door wide and settled in his armchair.

'We're going to have to lock him in again, aren't we?' I said.

'Has he had enough rum, though?' said Blum. He dumped the sack in the hedge. 'We'll go round and do it like last time.'

Five minutes later we were creeping up to the side of Mustard's shed. Blum stopped and picked up a tall piece of plywood, splashed and stained with concrete. He whispered to me, 'You nip and bolt the old bugger in.'

I nodded as we advanced. I went to the corner of the shed, grasped the door and slammed it shut. I scrabbled to get the bolt home, but fumbled. A bellow of indignation blasted from inside the shed. In my panic I fumbled again and felt a push at the door. I threw my whole, but puny weight against the pinewood planks and an instant before the next push, slid the bolt home. I backed away, shaking, to see Blum cover the side window by leaning the board against it.

Inside, Mustard Lugs was roaring. 'Let me out…I'll have the bloody police on yer… I'll leather your bloody arses.'

The planks of the door bulged as he pushed and pushed again.

I hissed to Blum, 'It's not going to hold.'

Mustard bellowed and hammered the door, 'Open this door or I'll flog you from gunnels to bloody bilges, you mutinous landlubber scum.'

Blum whispered, 'Got any gloves with you?'

'Gloves?'

Blum was already hurrying towards the stacks of bricks. I followed and in moments we were heading back with armfuls of bricks. While Mustard Lugs cursed and bellowed, we built a wall smack up against the door and front of the shed. Mustard was not a small man and as his anger was fuelled by rum, we didn't stint on the bricks. We worked in silence and without stopping until the wall was higher than the door and four feet thick.

But still we had more work to do. We retrieved the sack. Blum pulled out bamboo canes, some lengths of fence wire and two pairs of his mam's nylon stockings. We improvised a couple of kid's fishing nets, with a pair of nylons spare to cover any emergency.

We hurried to the ponds. Already the water levels were at a dangerous low. The only advantage of this was that the taddies were concentrated into a small, deeper area. With the nets we scooped up hundreds and hundreds of them. Each net full was unloaded with care into the sack, which Blum had lined with soaking wet lawn clippings. Often we stopped scooping to pour more pond water over the sack's precious cargo.

By now, Mustard Lugs' angry outbursts had grown infrequent. We guessed he'd finished his rum and decided to take a rest. We were unable to relax, though. Our job was a race against time. We had no idea how long the taddies might live in damp grass, but they had no choice for at least another hour or more. Satisfied that we'd managed to get most of them from the two shrunken ponds, we looked at the flooded trenches. The pump had been turned off and there remained only a long pool of muddy water at the foot of the excavation.

I was reluctant about scooping tadpoles from the bottom of a five foot muddy trench, especially in my school clothes. I caught Blum's eye.

'It's got to be done,' he said.

He pulled off his tie and I followed his example. In a minute we'd put our school clothes aside. In only our underpants, we slithered into the footings trenches with our nets and scooped. I dreaded what we might find, but was overjoyed to watch the water drain out of my net to reveal a wriggling mass of living tadpoles. Blum whooped in delight as he rescued dozens more.

We scooped until we couldn't find any more and rinsed the survivors in pond water before transferring them to the sack. By the time we'd dressed and given the sack a through soaking, it was almost dark. We headed for our bikes, leaving Mustard Lugs and the asparagus farm silent.

*

WE MUST HAVE made an odd sight; two lads in school uniforms cycling through Ainsdale village in the dark, one with a dripping sack balanced on his crossbar. But on our eight-mile journey, nobody challenged us and we saw no coppers who might have been suspicious enough to imagine we were junior burglars.

We crossed the railway level-crossing and headed down towards the shore. We left the bikes in a clump of marram grass and headed for the sand hills. Our only experience of the beach here was on crowded, sunny days. At night, it was a different world. The tide was up and we could hear the distant sound of the waves on the sands. As we dropped down into a flat area between the high sand hills we saw our destination, its surface shining in the light of the risen moon.

Blum shone his bike lamp on the water of the seasonal pond and we saw thousands of natter jack tadpoles in the shallow water. We waded in and tipped out our sack. Gently, we moved our fingers through the pile of wet cuttings to release our refugee taddies into their new home. We watched as hundreds of them wriggled away in all directions. I was exhilarated at the thought we'd given them a second chance. At least some would escape the spread of bricks and concrete across our parish.

Blum snapped off the torch, 'Well, seeing we're here, like, we might as well have a proper blummin' paddle.'

In moonlight, we ran down through the sand hills and out across the hard, flat sands to the edge of the sea. We shed our school clothes again and waded deeper and deeper into the waves. Up to our necks in water we washed off the mud of the trench.

'I wonder if Mustard Lugs is having sweet dreams,' shouted Blum. We splashed each other and laughed until we were choking on the salt water of the incoming tide.

*

MUSTARD LUGS GAVE up his job as watchman after he was walled up in the shed and had to be rescued by the builders. Years later, the natter jack population on the Lancashire coast became one the most important in Britain. I'd like to think our mission to rescue those from the asparagus farm, the introduction of new blood, had something to do with that.

Two nights after Mustard Lugs quit his job, the earth shifter was destroyed by fire. Somebody drained diesel oil out of its tank and pushed a blazing brazier underneath it. I'd like to think Blum had nothing to do with that, but on the two occasions I challenged him about it, he grinned and said, 'Don't be daft.' The second time I laughed and left it at that.

The Last Joke on Uncle Walter

BLUM WAS A master of the practical joke. No matter how much time and effort were needed, for him it was always worthwhile. He was also a purist. He knew that often the joker's pleasure was more intense if the effect on his victim was left to the imagination. And for a time, the pleasure was multiplied tenfold if the victim was his Uncle Walter.

Though I often took part in these practical jokes, I became uneasy at times, for looking back, Uncle Walter was an undeserving target. I admit I enjoyed the fun of these pranks, but I became aware I was perhaps out-growing the unseeing cruelty of youth.

Uncle Walter was a quiet and simple man. He was tall and thin. All legs, as Blum's mam said. He shambled, rather than walked. His corduroy trousers flapped around those long legs and his gabardine jacket hung like a sack over a fence post. He was a few inches over six feet tall, from army surplus boots to greasy flat cap. His long face, mottled with broken blood vessels beneath grey side whiskers, testified to a life spent outdoors.

From the age of fourteen, Uncle Walter was a farm worker. Until his retirement, he spent the last thirty years at Abram's place on the back Altcar road. He had a talent for mechanics, but since finishing on the farm, his time was split between tending the garden and orchard at Blum's mam's house and working cash-in-hand to keep the gardens of the better-off locals in good order. He didn't have a lot to say about anything and kept himself to himself as he pedalled his Raleigh Roadster between jobs.

Walter spent most of his working years living rent free in a 'paddy house,' a term for a tied-house, which originated with the large numbers of Irish farm workers who migrated to our part of England, searching for work after the horrors of the potato famine. Walter stood to lose his home when it came time for retirement, so after Blum's father died, his mother invited her older, bachelor half-brother to live at May Bank View.

Why Blum saw his Uncle Walter as a target to undermine, I was never completely sure.

Perhaps it was to do with the time Blum failed to stop when seen by a policeman riding without lights. Sergeant Ainsworth had been informed and came to May Bank View to read the Riot Act. Blum's mam failed to see how such a boyish prank needed police action. Even when she was told Blum had done it twice -- same place, same officer. But Walter tried to replicate the role of Blum's father -- or, rather, grandfather -- and announced Blum was to stay in for a month. Blum looked Uncle Walter in the eye and told him that he'd leave the house whenever he pleased. If Uncle Walter wanted to stop him, he'd have to fight. Walter tried once. Blum's mam had to intervene for fear her half- brother was injured and suggested Walter should mind his own business.

Blum glowed at this re-adjustment of the pecking order and for long after treated Uncle Walter as the underdog. Often he would comment to his mam, or visitors like me, that Uncle Walter was going mad. His mam would tut, tut and tell him not to be daft, but Blum was persistent and never missed a chance to create an illusion of his uncle's insanity.

Often, he would misplace Walter's pocket watch, or wind it backwards or forwards. Other times he would take his uncle's clean shirts and crush them into the laundry basket, knowing his mam would make Walter iron them again. I saw him take painstaking care as he unearthed the peas his mam had asked Walter to plant and then revel in the reaction when later no pea shoots appeared and Walter's angry claims that he'd definitely sown them were met with ridicule by his half-sister. One September when Walter was making plum wine for Christmas, I tried to persuade Blum to reconsider his actions as he added masses of sugar to the fermenting vessels in the wash house. He knew they would blow the lids within hours and timed the exercise to coincide with his mam's decision to wash and dry every item of linen in the house. Afterwards, she wouldn't speak to Walter for a full week as she scrubbed at scores of vivid port-coloured stains. For me, that was a 'joke' too far.

One evening in early summer as I turned into the gate at May Bank View to meet Blum, Uncle Walter scooted off on his bike like a man in a hurry. Usually, he greeted me with a shy nod, but this time I was ignored. As Walter slung a long leg over the saddle and started to pedal, Blum appeared on the drive and called after him.

'Hurry up! Don't want them to die, do yer!'

He was much amused as we turned the opposite way and headed for the travelling fun fair which had pitched up on a field beside the canal. I asked what he'd done to Uncle Walter this time. Blum laughed and said, 'Nowt yet. I haven't worked it out.'

Then he told me about a conversation between his mam and Uncle Walter that teatime.

Walter had taken on a new gardening job with a family called Bagshaw. Mr. Bagshaw was a barrister and recently moved in to an Edwardian house not far from the Scottish Soldier pub. Bagshaw and his family had that morning left for a fortnight in Biarritz. Uncle Walter complained that while the Bagshaws were away in France, as well as normal garden duties, Mr. Bagshaw expected him to feed the collection of carp in the newly-commissioned garden pond.

'I'm a gardener, not a zookeeper,' he told his half- sister, 'The missus told me they were worth an 'undred pounds. What if they die? What if heron 'as 'em?'

Blum looked up from his assault on a bowl of apple crumble to listen.

'It's not your fault if it does,' said Blum's mam.

'It's not just that,' Walter said, 'He wants them fed just before dark, every day, just like he does.'

His mam tutted, 'Can't you just throw a bit of bread in when you're there in the afternoon? '

'He's got these special food pellet things and I have to measure 'em out just right.'

'Sound's daft to me', said Blum's mam, 'All that for a few fish.'

'He reckons they need just the right amount of feed. Summat about regularatin' growth, he says.' He looked at his sister with apprehension, 'When he gets back he says he'll be able to tell how much they've grown to a hair's breadth.'

'Go on, he's pulling your leg.'

Uncle Walter was earnest, 'No it's all scientific with him. I seen a book he left in the summer house.'

Blum told me he'd kept quiet, but noted his Uncle Walter seemed troubled at this new and unwanted responsibility.

Blum was subdued as we walked along the canal towpath. When we reached the track down to the fair where we could hear The Kinks at full volume and smell fried onions and hamburgers, I said, 'Well? Have you worked it out?'

'There's one or two things I need,' he grinned, 'Then I'll be ready.'

We slipped into the crowds and excitement of the fair and treated ourselves to candy floss, Coke and hot dogs as we met up with other lads, but failed to strike up conversation with girls from school, who seemed almost old enough to be our mothers in C&A frocks, lipstick and high heels. Girls we larked about with on school days now had eyes only for the muscled and tattooed hard knocks who rode the

Waltzer deck, hands on hips, chewing gum and winking and leering at everything in a skirt.

By the time me and Blum had a go on the rifle range, I'd forgotten all about Uncle Walter and his fish.

The fat stall keeper with a copper ring in his ear was keeping a close eye on us. I got one bull's-eye, but Blum put four out of five shots dead centre and won himself a live goldfish in a plastic bag of water. When Blum flicked him a tanner and requested yet another five pellets for the air rifle, the stall keeper seemed suspicious. He hadn't noticed Blum reverse the stall keeper's dishonest adjustment of the rifle's back sight after his first shot. Two minutes later, the fat crook was seething and Blum had won a second goldfish. Blum came up with another sixpence, but the stall keeper demurred. He snatched away the rifle and announced in fairground style, 'Don't hog the show now, lads. Give someone else a chance.'

Blum picked up his goldfish and gave the stall keeper a knowing look. Minutes later we were creeping past a diesel generator behind the rifle range and coconut shy. Blum had to shout over the roar of machinery when I asked him what he was up to. He told me we needed to stay late at the fair. It was close to midnight when we left for home. Blum clutched his third 'prize'-- a big sweet jar of water in which swam more than a dozen goldfish, courtesy of the shyster with the copper ear ring. We crept away through the shadows, both of us fearful at every step we'd be beaten up by muscle-bound Waltzer men.

*

TWO NIGHTS LATER I was behind the hothouse at the Bagshaws' house. With red brick walls covered in Boston ivy, it stood in an acre of exquisite gardens. It was a still evening and I could smell the scent of jasmine blossom, lilies and fresh-mown lawn. Blum lifted the cover on one of a pair of big rainwater butts and nodded for me to look inside. He sprinkled a few pinches of ant eggs on the surface and up came the group of fish we'd liberated from the rifle range.

'I still don't know what you're playing at,' I said.

Blum closed the lid of the water butt. 'Me Uncle'll be here any minute,' he said, 'All we have to do is watch. I was up here last night, but I just want to make sure what he's doing.'

I was no wiser as we pushed our way into the cover of a rhododendron bush. We had a clear view of the ornamental pond about fifteen yards away. Minutes later, a startled woodpigeon clattered out of the walnut tree near the back gate. We tensed at the squeak of the gate latch then rustling as Uncle Walter leaned his bike against the hornbeam hedge

Soon he crossed the lawn to the summerhouse, at this time of the year covered in hundreds of pink clematis flowers. Through the side window, we saw him dip a brandy glass into a paper sack. He held up the glass and squinted at the level of brown pellets inside. He brushed off a few with his forefinger to level the amount. Blum watched, taking in every step of the feeding routine. Uncle Walter left and ambled over to the pond. He stood at the edge and upended the brandy glass over the water. Even at that distance we could see the eruption of sleek, golden bodies boiling the water, jostling and butting to gulp down Mr. Bagshaw's special pellets.

Uncle Walter crouched close to the water, put aside the brandy glass.

'Watch this,' whispered Blum.

He struggled to contain his mirth as we watched Walter mouth the numbers as he counted the fish on the fingers of each hand. Satisfied, he stood up and returned the brandy glass to the summerhouse and left, his extra work done. As soon as the back gate closed, Blum pushed out of the rhododendron bush and retrieved a long bag from behind a fringe of drooping, yellow laburnum flowers. 'Time for a bit of fishing,' he said.

With Blum manning the landing net and me dangling a hook covered in bread paste at the end of a rod and line, we soon pulled out two of the Koi carp.

Blum admired one of them. 'There's fifteen of these, all about the same size.'

It was a gleaming, lithe version of the goldfish from the fair, but a full ten inches longer. Each carp was whisked away by Blum to its temporary home in the second water butt behind Mr. Bagshaw's hot house.

We repeated our fishing trip for several nights. On each visit we hooked two or three of the Koi carp and rehoused them in the second water butt, where Blum and me kept up their ration of the pellets and checked them each day. We resisted the temptation to watch Uncle Walter's subsequent feeding trips. He had good hearing for an old man and, had we been detected, Blum said, it would spoil everything

*

TOWARDS THE END of the Bagshaws' holiday, I was at the kitchen table at May Bank View helping Blum to eat the first of his mam's strawberries. Minutes before Uncle Walter had cycled off for his stint at the barrister's house. Blum's mam came in from the garden with a bunch of cornflowers.

Blum winked at me and asked his mam. 'What's up with Uncle Walter? He wouldn't touch the strawberries. He's just clammed up and all, won't say a blummin' word.'

'It's them fish,' she said, stripping leaves off stems and not disguising her irritation, 'He's worrying himself to death. He thinks herons are eating them.'

She laid the cornflowers on the wooden drainer and took a pair of scissors from a hook on the wall. Blum grinned at me. I had to put my hand to my mouth to stop a laugh.

'Is he sure?' Blum said, grinning behind his mam's back, 'Has he counted them?'

'Exactly what I said,' she replied, 'I've a good mind to go and count them myself. I can't be doing with him mooching round fretting about some show-off's pet fish.'

Blum glanced up at the clock, then out through the kitchen window where already moths danced on the other side of the glass.

'When are Mr. and Mrs. Bagshaw coming home?' he asked, his voice casual. His fingers drummed on his skull and I knew he was plotting his next move.

'Saturday morning', she said, intent on placing the cornflowers in a glass vase, 'I'll be glad when he doesn't have to bother about them stupid carp.'

Blum mimed to me the action of a fishing rod and reel and we slipped out of the kitchen. On the way, Blum pocketed the battery torch from the dresser shelf.

*

WE HID BEHIND a clump of cow parsley just inside the cart track alongside the Bagshaws' grounds and waited until Uncle Walter cycled past us in the thickening dusk. He stared glum-faced at the road, a man far from at ease.

'Tonight we take the last of them out, 'said Blum. He chuckled in anticipation. 'Just wait 'til he turns up tomorrow.'

The remaining four carp were by now overfed and a touch harder to entice to the hook with their full bellies. The moon was high over the beech trees that fronted the house when we left. Blum was content the final stage of the operation was complete.

Blum said goodnight and reminded me to be at his house that following evening, the last night before the Bagshaws' return. He walked off into the dark whistling to himself.

*

I SIPPED A mug of tea in the back parlour at May Bank View as Blum and me watched *Take your Pick* with Michael Miles and Bob Danvers-Walker on the black and white television. As the programme ended, I heard Uncle Walter's anguished voice in the kitchen, interrupted by Blum's mam.

Blum vaulted over the arm of the sofa and went to the kitchen door. I was right behind him.

'What do you mean, they've gone smaller? Don't be so daft!' Blum's mam said.

Uncle Walter insisted, 'It's true, I tell you!'

He paced the kitchen, squeezing his cap between his hands, up and down in front of the ironing board where Blum's mam had been interrupted.

He seemed embarrassed to see Blum and me.

'How can fish grow smaller, for Heaven's sake?' said Blum's mam.

Uncle Walter made to speak, hesitated, then, blurted out. 'Cross me heart and hope to die, I'm telling you, it's true'

'What's up?' asked Blum.

Blum's mam turned to us, exasperated. 'One minute he's telling me these carp are all disappearing, now he says they're all there, but they've grown smaller!'

Blum snorted a laugh. 'I told you he's going mad!'

Uncle Walter jabbed his finger at Blum. 'Don't you start! I know when I'm right!' Then pointed at his eyes, 'There's nowt wrong with my eyes. I tell you them fish are grown smaller.'

Blum pushed him a bit harder. 'It's all in your head! Now I know you're going round the bend!'

Uncle Walter was too flustered and emotional, to defend himself.

'Talk about a screw loose, 'Blum said, 'Growing smaller, ha'

Uncle Walter held up his finger and thumb, the ends two inches apart. His face was pure misery, 'They're only this big now!'

'How many times do I have to say it?' said Blum, 'He's gone doolally, off his blummin' rocker.'

Blum's mam turned to her son, her voice sharp, 'That's enough!'

Blum backed off. Uncle Walter turned away, wringing his cap like a dishcloth, his bottom lip quivering.

'You'll just have to let Mr. Bagshaw sort it out. At least none of them are missing.' said Blum's mam. She looked to us and rolled her eyes, shook her head, 'Even if they are smaller.'

Uncle Walter struggled inwardly, and then shuffled a step closer to the ironing board.

'Will you come with me, to tell Mr. Bagshaw?' Blum's mam was startled, 'Me?!'

'I can't tell him on me own,' Uncle Walter said. He looked for a moment like a child.

I felt for poor Walter at that moment. I steeled myself, my embarrassment and guilt urging me to step forward and confess everything we'd done, but Blum must have sensed this, for I felt a restraining hand on my forearm. In the following tense moments I resisted the urge.

'Please, Nancy,' Walter said.

Blum's mam regarded her half-brother in his misery and relented. 'All right, I suppose so,' she said, after a moment, 'Mind you, what he'll think of me running round after a grown man, I don't know.'

Uncle Walter nodded his thanks. Blum turned to me, bursting with suppressed laughter.

*

IN THE BAGSHAWS' garden, an hour after dawn that Saturday morning, Blum was cock-a-hoop at the success of his joke on Uncle Walter. I felt guilty still, but we were both too busy to discuss such things.

With my jeans rolled up over my knees I spent more than an hour with the net chasing fifteen small goldfish round what now seemed more like a lake than a pond. Blum, meanwhile, was wishing for longer arms as he captured the same number of bigger, but equally elusive, Koi carp from inside the water butt. He carried them one at a time in wet sack cloth and returned them to their home.

*

WHILE UNCLE WALTER hoed the onion beds and we sat in the yard with mugs of tea, Blum quizzed his mam in detail about her visit to the Bagshaws' house.

She shook her head and rolled her eyes as she described what happened after interrupting the Bagshaws' late breakfast.

Walter couldn't face going to the pond and resumed his anxious cap-wringing as Mr. Bagshaw escorted Blum's mam across the lawn. Mr. Bagshaw, dressed in a brown linen suit and Panama hat, listened as Blum's mam explained that her half-brother was overwrought with the worry that something wasn't quite right with the fish.

'Um…What exactly makes him think that?' Mr. Bagshaw said.

Blum's mam was awkward, 'Well, he, he thinks they might…that they might not be growing properly.'

Mr. Bagshaw nodded, puzzled. He excused himself and brought the brandy glass full of pellets from the summerhouse. Uncle Walter advanced across the grass and watched at a distance. Blum's mam glared at him, embarrassed, as with sweating hands Walter twisted his cap even more.

Mr. Bagshaw tipped the glass of pellets into the pond. In an instant, the surface boiled with greedy ten-inch long fish. Uncle Walter stared in disbelief. Mr. Bagshaw watched the fish closely for a moment, then turned and beckoned to Uncle Walter.

Red-faced, Uncle Walter moved to join his half-sister and Mr. Bagshaw. His eyes never left the pond as the Koi carp swirled and butted each other to suck in the last pellets floating on the pond's surface.

Mr. Bagshaw smiled, 'They look splendid, Walter. Very healthy. Grown quite noticeably. You've done a sterling job, absolutely sterling.'

Walter nodded, mystified. His half-sister covered her relief.

'I'll go and ask Veronica to do some fresh coffee for us. Please go and sit on the terrace.'

Mr. Bagshaw smiled again and strolled back to the house.

Uncle Walter pointed at the carp and hissed, 'They was smaller, I'm telling yer!'

'That's enough of that,' said Blum's mam.

'It's true!'

Blum's mam was having none of it. 'I said, that's enough!'

*

TWO NIGHTS LATER, I helped Blum clip his father's prized yew hedge as Uncle Walter came down to the big greenhouse to water the tomato plants. Blum nodded for me to follow and we crept after him.

We hid behind the firewood store as Uncle Walter picked up a watering can and moved to the big galvanised tank which stored rain water from the greenhouse roof. He pushed the can into the tank and heaved it out full. He turned away. Then his head shot back, his face a snapshot of surprise. He peered into the tank and pushed his cap back on his head. He rubbed his eyes, staring into the water.

'I wondered where they went,' I whispered.

Blum was bursting with merriment. He dragged me away and we ran to the far end of the garden before collapsing on the grass, laughing until we couldn't laugh anymore. When he stopped laughing, Blum told me he had played his last practical joke on his Uncle Walter.

As far as I know, he kept his word and at Uncle Walter's funeral one raw winter's day when I returned from my job in a distant town, I watched at the graveside as Blum put his arm around his mam's shoulders and tears ran down his face.

A Bullet for Abel Jones

BLUM EXHALED A stream of fag smoke and let the sandbag take the weight of the heavy rifle. In the still and misty November air we could hear the sound of fireworks and smell the bad-egg stink of burnt gunpowder.

Blum raised himself up off his belly and sat up. He was impatient, 'Jeezus, why won't the old bugger settle himself?'

I looked at the lit scullery window a hundred yards away. A figure in shirt sleeves, his braces distinct against his blue, collarless shirt, moved from left to right and back again. Between him and us was a small strip of waste ground and the long gardens behind a terrace of four cottages. An end one belonged to Abel Jones. Unaware of our presence, he washed and dried his supper pots.

Blum ground out the butt of his Player's Cadet on the flat roof of the shed and flicked it into the darkness of Mrs. Davenport's back garden. Nobody knew we were there, including the owner, who was well into her seventies and deaf.

Smoke trickled from his mouth as he picked up the Great War field glasses which once belonged to his grandfather and focused them on the moving figure.

'Come on,' Blum said, 'Time to light your pipe, you old bastard.'

A rocket screamed up from somewhere behind us. It exploded above and the cascade of light caused us to duck down for fear of being seen. I was so nervous, each of the bang, bang, bang, bangs at its crescendo made me twitch.

Blum returned the field glasses to his eyes, 'We need a few more of them rockets, loud as you like.'

'Are you sure about this?' I said.

Even for Blum it was a reckless plot. One mistake could be disastrous. We could even end up charged with murder.

Blum lowered the glasses and faced me. 'Abel Jones stole your rod, didn't he?'

'I know he did, but…'

'But nowt, 'said Blum, 'He blummin' deserves it.'

He turned away and again lay on his belly. He pulled the butt of the rifle to his shoulder and adjusted it on the bags, so it pointed to the scullery window. Not so long ago I wanted Abel Jones to burn in hell, but now I wasn't too sure. I watched the distant figure continue to wipe and put away his pots and forced myself to rekindle the fury I felt months before when he stole my ten-foot, greenheart fishing rod.

*

IN THE MID-Sixties, Abel Jones was nearly seventy. He worked on the coal barges for years, but he'd been sacked for theft and was now retired.

He was well-known as an angler, but most of all as a teller of tall stories to anyone he met -- mostly to gullible lads from the parish. I'd been one of them. Blum, though, was not so easily convinced and sometimes -- to the old man's irritation -- laughed in his face. Behind his back, he called Jones 'The Liar.'

I can't remember all of Jones's ridiculous tales, but there are some that linger: like the winter his hands froze to the tiller of a barge and stuck fast all night, the time he rescued Lord Derby when he fell into the lock at Burscough and the thundery evening he saw an eel as thick as a man's thigh slither out of a cabbage field into the cut at Haskayne. Not to mention the day he killed a mighty pike.

Abel Jones added to his old age pension in various ways. He sold fruit and flowers from his garden and eggs from his hens. Throughout the fishing season, he sold home-made floats cut from peacock quill, split shot and ready-made casts, each complete with a hook, float and weight and wrapped around a notched strip of thin fruit box wood. These were sold to local lads like me and Blum. For the right price, he could repair fishing rods and make them like new and he bred maggots to sell for bait, fattening them on pig heads hung, stinking, inside old dustbins at the end of his garden. In fine weather you'd find him in his shed by the vegetable patch; on cold or wet days he'd be in the scullery, where the tackle was laid out on a table under the window, covered not in a cloth, but the pages of the previous week's Thursday *Advertiser*.

If Jones was out, he'd be on duty as a part-time bank warden for the waterways board. With control over four miles of the cut, it was his job to sell and check fishing licenses and to enforce the board's bureaucratic angling rules. If you played the game, you'd get advice -- and tall tales. If you didn't, you might have your fishing gear confiscated -- or, if your face didn't fit, be 'had up' before the magistrates and fined two pounds. Those fishing without a licence and no cash even for a 'day ticket' learned to keep one eye on the float and one on the towpath for the approach of an old man in a grey tweed jacket and trilby riding a bike with a basket on its handlebars -- the signal to leg it, or hide your gear.

That was the mistake Blum and I made that afternoon on the opening day of the angling season. We were both so intent on my float we didn't notice Abel Jones' approach. I was pleased with my new greenheart rod. One of my uncles found it when he moved into a house in Liverpool and cleared the attic. My dad spent hours showing me how to strip off its peeling varnish, re-whip the rings with cotton and re-varnish the whole rod. Equally, I was pleased with the little perch and six small roach I'd landed. I felt my new rod was bringing me luck, which made a change.

I was never a dedicated angler. Like smoking fags and drinking beer later on, I tried it because all the lads did, but I never became addicted—not to fishing, anyway. With Blum it was different. Angling was in his blood.

His father had fished most weekends in season from when he was a lad until the Saturday before he died, without warning, when Blum was ten. Since he could walk, Blum had accompanied his father countless times to pits, meres, rivers and all along the canal. One autumn morning on the parish boundary at Downholland, Blum left his float-fished maggot in the water while his father unravelled the line from around the ring at the tip of Blum's bamboo rod. Blum prepared to cast out again and found he was battling a three-pound roach. He was seven-years-old. Never again did he catch a roach close to that specimen size. But he never gave up on the hope he would.

Like his father, Blum turned up his nose at fishing matches. Filling a keep net with tiddlers and weighing them in for a cash prize was not his idea of fishing. He wanted quality, not quantity; a specimen fish, rather than a silver cup. Blum never broke any records, but I saw him land some nice fish; once a plump crucian only a quarter-pound short of the British record.

On the day of my run-in with Abel Jones, I was happy to catch tiddlers while Blum urged me to fish deeper to try to connect with one of the canal's dinner-plate sized bream. Blum wasn't fishing that day. His Uncle Walter was confined to bed by Dr. Grey and Blum spent the morning helping his mam catch up on work in their big garden. We were unaware of Abel Jones until we heard tyres brake behind us on the towpath cinders.

'Let's see your licence, lad,' he said, as we turned away from the water and saw him astride his bike.

I didn't know what to say, or do, I had no full-season permit, or even a day-ticket, but Blum was straight in. 'Lovely day to start the season.'

'Grand,' said Abel Jones.

'Anyone catching much?' said Blum, 'Anyone had a tench out yet?'

Jones nodded back along the cut to Pilling bridge, 'Feller back yon's had a couple, maybe a pound and a bit each.'

'Nobody's ever had a decent size'un on this stretch, not tench,' Blum said.

I realised Blum was building a smokescreen, to distract Jones from the matter of my licence.

'I've had a dozen, or more, decent tench out in me time,' said Jones.

'Nothing big, though,' Blum said. Or rather, he stated it as fact.

Abel Jones was irked by the remark, 'None of 'em less than five pound.'

Blum laughed, 'Ha, five pound tench? In here?'

Abel Jones pointed at the water. His tone of voice had an edge, 'Listen to me, lad. There's tench bigger than that in there. I mightn't have caught them, but you see things on the boats. I've seen tench damn near a yard long. Eighteen pound, twenty pound, maybe bigger.'

'The record's only seven and a half, isn't it?' Blum said, 'My dad fished this cut all his life. If there were double-figure tench he'd've told me.'

Abel Jones regarded Blum.

'Eric Gatley was your old man, wasn't he?' said Jones.

Blum nodded. 'That's right.'

'I thought so.' he said, 'Maybe he got mixed up about what he said and what he didn't, eh? It's been known.'

I didn't follow Jones' odd remark. Blum eyed the bank warden for a moment or two, but said nothing. He made a move to leave.

'Let's try up at Pilling bridge,' he said.

I went to pass Jones, but he stuck out his arm. 'Ey, up, lad, I haven't seen your ticket.'

'I, erm, I forgot to get one,' I said.

Jones reached in his pocket for his day ticket pad and pen. 'That'll be one and six.'

I'd spent the last of my money on a spool of nylon line. I didn't have a penny. I looked to Blum, but he grimaced and shrugged. I turned back to Jones, 'I've no money on me,'

Blum butted in. 'He can drop it off at yours first thing, can't he?'

'No money, no ticket. No ticket, no fishing,' said Jones.

'I promise I'll pay tomorrow,' I said.

'Not allowed,' said, Abel Jones, his hand out, 'Give us that rod.'

I was desperate, 'I promise I'll pay, honest.'

'The rod, if you don't mind,' said Jones.

With my feelings of resentment bubbling up, I handed him the rod and he bit off the cast, reeled in the line and pulled it in to three sections. 'Nice bit of greenheart, that,' he said. Then added, 'I'm confiscating this in my capacity as bank warden.'

I was upset, 'But I've only just got it. You can't take it. It's not fair.'

'Rules is rules, you should've thought on,' he said. 'Another thing an' all, you're banned off the cut for the rest of the season.'

This was unbelievable, unheard of in our experience. I protested, 'But it's only the first day.'

Blum butted in, 'If he packs up now, you can give him another blummin' chance, can't you?'

He ignored both of us as he put my rod sections across the front of his handlebar basket, then warned me, 'I see you fishing on here you'll be 'ad up.' He faced Blum, 'I'll be watching you an' all, Gatley. One step out of line and you're banned.'

Then he cycled away.

I was on the edge of tears as I kicked at a tussock of grass and lashed my worms and bread paste into the water.

Blum said, 'You'll not see that rod again. He'll sell it tonight in the Hare and Hounds, the thieving bastard.'

In impotent anger I watched Abel Jones cycle away towards Bell's Lane and wished him dead.

*

NOW, ON THE roof of Mrs. Davenport's shed, the thing I feared most was Abel Jones' death.

Blum flicked away another cigarette end. 'No more cigs until I've taken the shot,' he said, 'Army snipers never smoke for a full day before they shoot, you know. Makes 'em shaky, like, so they say.'

That did little to help my anxiety. Blum was a good shot with a shotgun, or an air rifle. I'd seen him nail a pair of springing teal ducks with two shots from his stolen four-ten shotgun, as well as a zigzagging snipe we put up from a ditch. With an air rifle, he could shoot a dried pea off a fence rail at twenty paces and a slinking rat at dusk was an easy mark. But after his chain-smoking the past hour, I was anxious that like some other sniper, the procession of tonight's fags may have destroyed his marksmanship too.

We heard the squeak and rattle as the distant scullery window opened. Abel Jones lowered the top half of the sash. We'd watched his movements after dark for the past few nights. After washing the dishes, he would switch on the radio and open the window to allow out his pipe smoke. Then he would settle to make floats, repair a rod, or assemble his ready-made casts at the table under the window. By nine o'clock at the latest, he would get his hat and coat and cycle to the Hare and Hounds.

Blum shifted his position behind the rifle and bag. I thought back to my first inkling of Blum's plot against Abel Jones. In an act of solidarity with me over my ban, Blum had not fished the cut since June. Although the theft of my greenheart rod marked the start of the long, slow decline in my enthusiasm for angling, we continued to fish, but only in the many old, flooded marl pits you could find in almost any field in the parish and beyond, where no licence was needed in those days.

One muggy day at the end of the summer holidays, we were fishing for perch at the two-acre Hill House Pit. As I reeled in a four-ouncer on my old bamboo rod, the fish was hit by the arrow strike of a jack pike. In turn, I struck, hoping to hook the jack as well, but the little pike won and swirled back into the depths carrying my perch.

Blum laughed, 'Ha, too blummin' slow.'

'Sodding hook's too small anyway,' I said.

'You should've shot the bugger,' said Blum. He grinned, 'Like that bloody liar, Abel Jones.'

I laughed. How many times had we heard that story? It must have been at least half a dozen. We'd heard it a time or two as well when the audience had been made up of a group of younger anglers who happened to be in Abel Jones' scullery. The last time was, the year before, we'd called in to buy maggots and had to wait while Jones finished the tall tale about catching his biggest pike.

We stood sneering and grinning at each other as Abel Jones told the boys how he had tried to catch the pike in a flooded quarry.

'I was after that devil for near six months,' he said,' Snagged him twice, but both times he shook the hook out. Danced across the water on his tail, he did, shaking his head like a mad dog. Me rod were doubled over.'

We stifled our merriment as he went on,' Well, summat had to be done. It'd eaten all the fish in that delph and now it was eating the ducklin's from the farm. The Missus at the farm wouldn't leave me alone 'til I had that pike out. She told me it were worth a pound note if I could kill that monster by the end of the week.'

Blum shifted and gave a theatrical yawn. I sniggered. Abel Jones flashed us a dirty look as the little lads waited on his tall tale.

'Well, I were down there by dawn the next day. I had a nice juicy gudgeon fish stuck on a treble hook. That pike took it in a flash, hooked him instant, like. Off he went, but he didn't know my plan, did he? Soon as he came up and started that dance malarkey, I reached in my pocket and pulled out this…'

Jones' hand shot out to the shelf beside him and grabbed a little, nickel-plated revolver. We'd seen it all before, but the lads swapped excited looks at the sight of the six-shooter.

Abel Jones aimed the revolver towards the scullery floor, 'I took aim as he started to shake his head and -- bang! -- I plugged him. Stone dead on the end of me line, he was, and I carried him up to the farm and got me quid.' The boys were in awe as Abel Jones clicked the pistol's chambers and then blew from the muzzle a wisp of imaginary gun smoke.

In the warm sunshine beside the pit, Blum laughed as we remembered the the story. 'Didn't mention it was a titchy little pin-fire revolver from Froggy Land, did he? Sort of thing some French tart'd keep in her handbag.'

He snorted, and added, 'Didn't blummin' mention you couldn't hit a cow's arse with it from two steps away, either, the bloody liar.'

Later, as we continued to fish the pit, I noticed he was tapping his head, his usual signal that some plot was being hatched and evaluated. I knew, too, that I'd find out what it was only when Blum was ready.

*

ABEL JONES WASN'T mentioned between us until weeks later. I called at Blum's house one Saturday in October and was surprised when his mam said he was at the library. A library wasn't Blum's choice of venue any day of the week and I was intrigued. I biked down the canal towpath and found him hunched over a book in the reading room.

'What are you doing in here?' My voice was too loud. A librarian with an armful of novels paused and glared at us over her glasses.

Blum grinned and put his finger to his lips. In a whisper, he said, 'I'm swotting up. Never thought you'd see that, did you? He laughed, 'I need a bit of information.'

He pulled a duffel bag from under his chair and handed it to me. 'Have a look in there.'

I opened the bag and went to take out the object inside.

His voice was a hiss, 'Not in here!'

I sat down and peered inside. It was a black and red tin, like a little paint tin, with a tattered label which read. 'Curtis's and Harvey's Black Powder.' It was gunpowder, the genuine stuff.

I checked over my shoulder for ear- wiggers. My voice was hushed, I was impressed, 'Where did you get it?'

'Mam asked me to go next door to get some coal in for Mr. Gidlow. It was there on the blummin' shelf in his outhouse, just asking to be borrowed.'

'You mean you swiped it?'

'What use is a tin of that stuff to someone who's blummin' ninety?'

It was a fair point, but Blum had always had an odd attitude to theft. He'd steal the cross from the altar of the parish church if it was required for one of his jokes, or to get back at someone, yet I'd seen him go to endless lengths to return dropped coins and lost umbrellas to their owners. Once he searched for weeks to return a penknife to a fellow angler when the only fact he knew about the man was he worked as a car mechanic not far from Southport. Other times, he took what he wanted without conscience. Whatever he stole, he could always justify the act.

I waited another half an hour as Blum made notes from the book. We cycled back up the canal bank.

'What are you going to do with it?' I said, 'You could make a load of bangers, a bomb even.'

'Nah, we're going to get our own back on Abel Jones,' he said. 'Thing is, it depends on whether Captain Westbrook sticks to his routine.'

I was puzzled. Captain Westbrook was a retired army officer who lived on his own not far from Blum's house. Blum's mam was a seamstress, but also worked as a cleaning lady for several locals, including the Captain, for whom she was a part-time housekeeper. I was sure the Captain wasn't a friend, or even an acquaintance, of Abel Jones.

'What's he got to do with it?'

'You'll see,' said Blum.

'What about Abel Jones? What are you going to do to him?'

Blum grinned and tapped his nose. 'It depends. Just make sure you're not up to your eyes in that blummin' Latin homework of yours, not round Bonfire Night.'

*

ON HALLOWEEN NIGHT, I was with Blum when he pocketed a key from the kitchen dresser drawer at May Bank View. His mam and Uncle Walter were watching *The Avengers* on telly. A few minutes later Blum turned the key in the lock of Captain Westbrook's back door. The Captain was away on his annual visit to his sister's home in St. Albans. Each year he combined the stay with a reunion dinner with former army colleagues at a hotel in the West End.

On the way, Blum told me the reason for the Captain's involvement in his plans. He was among the first battalions of the British army to enter Hitler's Germany at the end of WWII. As an officer, it was part of his duties to oversee the confiscation and destruction of firearms held by German civilians. Even hunting guns and those for shooting targets had to be destroyed.

One day, the Captain ordered his men to lay hundreds of shotguns and rifles crossways along the kerbstones of a road outside a small town. He then had an army lorry move slowly along the kerb to crush the guns, to render them useless.

'What a blummin' waste of guns, eh?' said Blum, leading the way into the hallway, switching

123

on lights, 'The Captain said it were heart-breaking. People's prized possessions; lovely German craftsmanship; all being destroyed in minutes. Anyway, Captain Westbrook spotted this rifle, couldn't bear to see it buggered-up, so he stopped the lorry and nabbed it.'

Blum opened a door off the hallway and switched on the light. We went inside the Captain's study. It had a green leather armchair and Chesterfield sofa and a desk and chair. Blum pointed to the back wall over the sofa. A rifle hung on hooks. 'He brought it back with him after the war. It's a Scheutzen, a muzzle-loading percussion lock target rifle.'

I moved closer to the rifle. It was a strange looking gun, decorated with leaves and fancy patterns on the wood and the metal. It had a deep, odd-shaped stock with an iron hook at its heel to tuck into the shooter's armpit. Under its barrel was a pipe containing a ramrod and there was a round wooden knob on a stick which was screwed into the woodwork in front of the trigger. At the back was a complicated looking, adjustable sight with knurled knobs. It had a swan's neck hammer like an old-fashioned shotgun.

Blum reached up and removed it from the polished wooden gun hooks. 'It weighs a ton and all, but it's dead accurate.'

'How do you know?'

'The Captain told me. He wasn't supposed to fire it, but he couldn't resist. He got hold of a bit of gunpowder and some percussion caps and tried it out down the back lawn. That reminds me…'

He passed me the rifle. It was so heavy I almost dropped it.

Blum was at the Captain's desk opening drawers. 'What are you doing?'

He opened another drawer, 'If I'm wrong on this we've had it. '

As Blum rooted, I tried to aim the rifle at a photograph of a young Captain Westbrook in a frame on top of a tallboy. It was a struggle to hold it still in a shooting position. I managed to keep it on aim for a couple of seconds before I had to let it down. I heard a metallic rattle.

Blum beamed and held up a small round tin. In his other hand was a drawstring bag.

'Bingo! Eley Number 11 Percussion Caps and some lead balls. I had a feeling the Captain might've hung on to these.'

*

NEXT MORNING FOUND us at Pygon's Farm, where nobody had lived since old Dick Seddon's wife died and he hanged himself; where a farmer was once eaten alive by his pigs. While Blum prepared the German rifle for its first shot, I paced out a hundred yards in the pasture and used clout nails to fix a cardboard target to the trunk of a goat willow tree. We were anxious strange sounding shots might be investigated, but when Blum propped the rifle on a pile of rotting straw bales and fired off the first lead ball it sounded little different to a shotgun. It chucked out a fair cloud of smoke, mind.

Blum referred to his notes from the library as alternately he fired off shots and scrubbed burnt powder from the barrel. The rifle took a couple of minutes to load as a measured charge of powder had to be dropped down the barrel before a lead ball wrapped in cotton shirt material was rammed home on top of it. After two hours he had the hang of the gun and had set the sights to suit the distance. There was enough gunpowder left for one shot. As Blum said, it was a one shot job. There would be no second chance.

Blum decided that the best time to use the rifle against Abel Jones was Bonfire Night when a shot close to houses after dark would be dismissed as a firework.

*

BY EIGHT O CLOCK on November the fifth, fireworks filled the sky as I looked through the field glasses at Abel Jones and Blum squinted through the tiny hole in the rear sight of the German rifle. Abel Jones, pipe in his mouth, was sitting at his table. While tobacco smoke curled around him then left through the open window, he painted the tips of quill floats with red paint.

'Do you reckon he's sitting still enough?' said Blum.

'I'd say so.'

My heart was racing. I hoped Blum's wasn't. This shot had to be true. The planned path of the round lead bullet was about eighteen inches above Abel Jones' bald head. At a hundred yards a slight movement by Blum as he squeezed the rifle's trigger could alter the flight of the bullet by feet, never mind inches. A tiny error in his execution of the shot could mean Abel Jones got a bullet between his eyes.

Blum spoke to himself. 'Breathe in…' Another rocket screeched into the smoky air above us. 'Breathe out, breathe in and…'

Blum stopped breathing. I lowered the field glasses and glanced at his hand as the pad of his forefinger rested on the trigger. I tore my eyes away from the rifle and looked back at Abel Jones and his paintbrush through the field glasses. I shifted them slightly higher to observe the target.

Abel Jones' finest fish ever was that quarry pike of twenty-seven pounds. It was the only fish he ever had cast by a professional taxidermist. The deep-bellied monster with its faded green flanks and yellow spots hung on a polished mahogany board on the back wall of the scullery.

There was a whooshing thump of a report as the rifle trigger broke, the cap ignited the charge of gunpowder and the ball set off on its flight path towards Abel Jones' window. It seemed like a second's delay then the plaster pike on the wall exploded and atomised into white dust. A millisecond later I lost sight of Abel Jones as the dust cloud filled the room and poured out of the open window.

'That's how to shoot a pike, you bloody liar,' Blum shouted as gunpowder smoke billowed around us and fireworks banged, whizzed and crackled across the sky. Our tension dissolved into uncontrollable laughter.

*

WE WERE STILL breaking into spontaneous fits of laughter the next night. Captain Westbrook's souvenir of the war was cleaned, oiled and back on his study wall, now retired for good after its successful mission. I was round at May Bank View. Blum's mam spread jam on the toast she'd made for us.

'Thank Heavens those fireworks are over for another year,' she said, 'Do you know some idiot put a banger through Mrs Knightley's letterbox? It's just not funny; the state of her heart, she could've died of fright.'

She glanced at us,' I hope you two wouldn't do anything dangerous like that.'

'Don't be daft,' said Blum.

She put our plates of toast on the table, 'I heard in the shop Abel Jones had a rocket through his back window as well. It caused all sorts of mess. Could've killed him, he said.'

We swapped a look, grinning at each other.

'Ha,' said Blum, 'He's a liar, always has been.'

'Oh, I know that all right, 'said his mam.

'You've heard his tall stories, then?' I said.

'I don't know about tall stories, but I do know he's a liar.'

She hesitated for a moment, and then decided to say more.

'I don't really like to talk about it, but when Mr. Gatley was foreman at the feed mill Abel Jones stole bags of chicken corn off the quayside and got six months in prison.'

I looked at Blum. He nodded confirmation.

Blum's mam said, 'He tried to wriggle out of it and said Eric told him he could help himself and they'd share the money. It was a wicked lie. Eric said no such thing and he almost lost his job. He would've done if the owner's father hadn't stepped in. He vouched for Eric's honesty to the police.'

She shook her head.

'It was a terrible time for us, a real worry with me-laddo there on the way.'

She moved away to fill the kettle and I saw Blum's eyes go to the framed photograph on the dresser. It was Blum's mam and dad on their wedding day in the 1940s. His eye glistened as he regarded his mother and dead father in happy times.

I realised my greenheart fishing rod wasn't the only reason he took that grave risk and fired a bullet through Abel Jones' scullery window.

The Silent Feud

HARRY CATLOW AND Charlie Abram were the tenants of neighbouring farms, but for most of their lives they never spoke a word to each other. It was a silent feud.

It wasn't as if the two farmers went out of their way to avoid each other. For apart from Christmas Day and Easter Sunday, they faced each other across the bar of the Plough Horse every day of the year.

Harry would stand in the taproom and Charlie in the parlour, a bare six feet of mahogany counter top and bar space between them. But never a word was exchanged; no greetings, or even a nod to acknowledge the other's presence or, indeed, existence.

It was rare, too, for either man to speak to any other customer, both being content with their drink and their own company. In those days they were known as 'topers,' but these days they'd be diagnosed as drink dependent or even functioning alcoholics.

The reason why the two men fell out so badly they denied each other's existence for decades was lost. What was known, though, is that it ignited a furious and bloody fist fight between them; one that saw both men maimed. Harry Catlow's nose was never the same again and Charlie Abram's right ear healed as a shapeless lump of flesh and gristle.

It was said that Harry Catlow started to drink when he was five years old. Local legend had it he sampled an Irish farm worker's pint at a wedding party at Catlow's Farm before the Great War and got the taste. Charlie Abram was rumoured to have suffered violence from his father and, after years of passive acceptance, had one night drunk ten bottles of barley wine at the Scottish Soldier, then gone home to break his father's ribs and beat him unconscious. The older man died a few months later and some said Charlie was so overcome with guilt he took to drink.

My grandmother once ran the village shop and often told me of things she'd heard about local families. She believed the farmers' fisticuffs and feud were to do with money, but she could provide no details. Another theory suggested the two farmers fell out over a girl. That was possible as they were said to be handsome as young men and both were in line to inherit substantial farm tenancies.

A third suggestion I heard claimed their rift as young men stemmed from an act of cowardice in the North African campaign in World War II. The teller of the tale went into fanciful detail about Catlow and Abram fighting a duel in the sands of the Libyan desert.

My dad laughed aloud at the idea. He told me that a one-time landlord of the Plough Horse once informed him the fight took place outside the pub, years before the war, he couldn't recall when. The same publican said he would have barred them for life had the fight erupted inside. Both men had continued to visit the pub, he said, as both were too stubborn to lose face. Neither the publican, nor my dad, ever found out what the fight was about.

Many years later, these theories were debated by Blum and me one school summer holidays as we idled a day away fishing and smoking fags at the canal bridge by the Plough Horse. Our discussion was prompted when Charlie Abram's Jaguar car rumbled across the planks of the swing bridge and turned down the sloping cobbled forecourt of the pub.

Abram braked an instant too late for there was a loud crunch of metal on brick as the front of the Jag made contact with the wall of the Plough Horse. We hurried along the bank for a better look and were amused to see Abram get out of the car, straighten his tie and smooth down his tweed jacket, then head for the front door without even checking the damage to his vehicle.

Blum laughed, 'He doesn't give a bugger about his cars – Never 'as.'

As he spoke, we heard the sound of a tractor. Harry Catlow at the wheel of an old, grey Fordson, splattered with dried mud, drove up the lane at speed. Catlow braked hard and wrenched at the wheel, slewed his vehicle down the cobbles and switched off the engine. Bang on noon, he pulled around himself the army greatcoat he wore winter and summer and swung himself from the driver's seat, down on to the cobbles. While Abram had turned right into the pub parlour, Catlow, spat, crossed the small lobby and entered the taproom.

We left our tackle and crossed the canal bridge to look at the Jag. The impact had smashed the front nearside indicator and head light and crumpled the surrounding royal blue metalwork. A nearby dent in the bonnet had already rusted where paint peeled following an earlier prang.

It was true Abram was careless with his vehicles. Everyone in the parish had seen the evidence. His previous green Jag had been replaced after collisions with a wall on the main road, a parked bread van and the machinery in his own farmyard. A Humber Snipe was once written off the day he bought it when he needed to speak with one of his sons and drove it at speed across twenty acres of fresh plough, the gearbox screaming, and Charlie too drunk to recall the field was divided by a ten foot deep ditch. Charlie never owned a car for more than a few months and the locals had seen a procession of brand new Fords, Austins and other makes abused by his drunken driving. In those pre-breathalyser days, he'd been fined, but not banned for driving under the influence. No lessons were learned from his court appearances and still he drove no matter how much he'd had to drink.

Whether Harry Catlow had been involved in any drunken driving accidents, we didn't know. Now and then he was seen driven by the Missus in a spotless Austin A40, but his usual transport was the Fordson, which he drove at top speed on the public highway. Harry's 'Chariot,' as the regulars called the Fordson, spent almost as much time parked up in front of the pub as it did elsewhere, for Harry

Catlow never missed a dinnertime, tea-time or evening session. Charlie Abram tended not to visit the Plough Horse late evening, possibly he was too drunk to drive by then, but had an immaculate attendance record for dinner and teatime.

While I ran my hand over the Jaguar's fresh wounds, Blum called me. I looked as his hand snaked through the open window and took the key and its fob from the ignition.

He tossed the key in his hand, 'Wonder what he'd do if I lobbed it in the cut?'

I laughed. It was a nervous laugh as I knew Blum would chuck it in if he felt like it. 'Probably go and buy a new car,' I said.

'Not much point then.' He opened the door and pulled up the floor mat. He put the key on the floor of the car and replaced the mat.

He grinned and closed the door, 'Let's see what happens, eh? '

We shifted our fishing rods and bait so we had a good view of the front of the pub. We discussed the theories about the feud. Was it about money? Or a girl? Or was it about something even more serious? An hour or so later, Charlie Abram walked with a slight sway out of the front door. He got into the car. For a few minutes he looked about and then sat immobile in the Jag. Minutes passed.

'Ha, you can see his blummin' brain ticking over,' said Blum.

The door of the Jag opened and Charlie Abram got out. He left the door wide open and went back inside the pub.

I laughed, 'Bet he'll be in there 'til closing time now.'

'Aye, he won't move till they shut the tap off,' said Blum.

We were wrong. Well before afternoon closing, a Massey Ferguson tractor pulled up alongside the Jag. It looked like a call had been made for help. A man in his twenties we recognised as Charlie Abram's younger son left the tractor engine running and strode into the Plough Horse. A minute later, he ushered out his protesting father.

The son went to the Jaguar and checked the ignition. He cursed and grumbled as he turned and started to go through his father's pockets. We were too far away to hear their exact words, but it was Charlie Abram's turn to curse as his son emptied the contents on to the roof of the Jag, silver and coppers spilling on to the cobbles.

Unable to find the ignition key, young Abram went around the car opening each door in turn and searching inside. He returned to the driver's door. A few moments later, as we sniggered, the younger man held up the missing key. He took hold of his dad's hand and thrust the key fob back into his possession. With a few shouted remarks, he returned to the Massey Ferguson. He reversed at speed and threw the vehicle round in a circle. We glimpsed his furious face before he accelerated away down the lane.

Charlie Abram stared at the key in his hand. At that moment, Harry Catlow came out of the pub, pressed his finger to one nostril and blew a stream of snot from the other in the direction of his one-time opponent. Without even a glance at Charlie Abram, he stumbled across the cobbles, climbed on to his Fordson and fired up the engine. Then he hurtled down the lane twice as fast as Abram's son.

Charlie Abram turned and watched him go before getting back into his car. We watched him reverse with the remaining three doors wide open. Heedless of the doors, he drove off, each of them slamming shut in turn as he gathered speed and veered from side to side and out of sight down the lane.

'I wish I knew what caused their fight,' I said, as we split Charlie Abram's dropped change between us.

Blum was reflective, 'I wonder if he thinks Harry Catlow hid his key.'

*

NEITHER OF US saw Harry Catlow or Charlie Abram until October. It was time for lifting late potatoes and most years our half-term holiday meant spud-picking. I had my eye on a dark blue reefer jacket I thought might impress a girl at the youth club. Blum needed a few quid to make an offer on a nine millimetre orchard gun for his collection of weaponry. Picking potatoes by hand was ten times tougher than picking anything else, bar cutting Brussels sprouts in a Christmas frost, but we knew we could earn twenty-five bob a day, cash in hand, for each back-breaking shift.

We'd picked spuds at Catlow's and Abram's in the past, but this time we opted for Catlow's, not least because we'd picked broad beans at Abram's place in July and Blum was caught packing his bean hampers with stones to boost their weight. His communist-like speech about sharing out the wealth Abram's farm reaped from a big Birds Eye frozen peas contract -- and the fact his Uncle Walter had sweated for the Abrams for most of his working life -- failed to impress Charlie Abram's eldest lad and we were both shown the gate.

We joined a group of others hopeful of work at Catlow's Farm at eight o' clock on the Monday morning. Like thirteenth century serfs, or even twentieth century dock workers, we watched the back hall entrance of the farm house for the appearance of Harry Catlow, who, in feudal fashion, would decide on the spot who worked that day and who trudged back up the lane.

While Charlie Abram lived in comfortable retirement thanks to two sons and his regular Birds Eye contract, Harry Catlow had no sons and no frozen peas contract. His two daughters had long since opted for city life, his landlords had reduced the farm's acreage by selling land for house building and Harry, with the Missus handling the paperwork, kept the place in slim profit with just a single hired man and constant seven-day working weeks, minus the hours spent at the bar of the Plough Horse. Lifting spuds, or praters, as the older folk called them, was done the labour-intensive way at Catlow's Farm

We stood in the frosty yard for ten minutes before we were alerted to Harry Catlow's appearance by the slam of a door and a fit of hacking coughs. He crossed the yard towards us, his army coat trailing behind black wellington boots, his filthy cap low over his eyes, a fag in his hand. He gobbed an oyster of phlegm on to the cobbles, wiped his running nose on his coat sleeve, and gave us would-be workers the once over. Without even a greeting, he pointed at individuals and said, 'Thee…thee… thee…' There was a communal tension as he paused. How many pickers did he want? Then a ragged cheer as he added, 'I'll take the lot o' thee. Get on that trailer.'

Out in the field the hired man had already made a start when Harry's Chariot pulling a trailer full of us spud-pickers arrived. After a swig of rum from the pewter flask in his greatcoat pocket, Harry Catlow got down off the tractor and shouted instructions. Most of us knew what he wanted and collected the big, square hamper baskets from the stack at the edge of the field.

The hired man's tractor carried a spinner, a device which was pulled behind at strolling pace. The revolving spinner broke open the raised rudges containing the potatoes. The spuds tumbled off the sides of the spinner and we followed, picking the unearthed crop and dropping them into our hampers. First time I went spud-picking it seemed easy work, but it doesn't take long before your back aches. It aches even more when you have to lug a full hamper basket to the patrolling trailer and lift and topple several stone of potatoes over its side. Your hands soon grow sore and go stiff with cold.

Dinner break was from noon to one o' clock. No whistle was needed to sound the start of the break for at five minutes to twelve, his rum flask empty, Harry Catlow aimed his Chariot in the direction of the Plough Horse and accelerated away. So keen was he to reach his destination, he didn't even uncouple the trailer, or stop at the yard to unload the spuds. On other days, he might be in the pub until three 'o'clock, but at drilling time, harvest, or spud picking, he would swallow as many pints of bitter as he could manage in an hour. We watched as the Fordson and trailer bounced down the track to the yard. Moments later we spotted it tearing up the lane, Harry Catlow crouched over the steering wheel like a jockey.

I pulled my corned beef butties out of my jacket pocket, as Blum laughed, 'Looks like he wants to get served before old Charlie.'

I expected to eat our carrying- out in the field, but Blum was keen to phone the seller of the orchard gun. He suggested a walk up the lane to the telephone box not far from the Plough Horse. It was better than suffering frozen feet, so I tagged along and we ate as we walked, noting at least a half-hundredweight of spuds scattered by Harry Catlow's breakneck, bouncing progress.

When Blum had made his call, we started back across the swing bridge to Catlow's spud field. Outside the Plough Horse we saw the Fordson tractor and trailer. Littered around it were yet more lost potatoes, witness to Harry Catlow's hard-braking arrival. That was no surprise, but the vehicle parked next to it was -- a new, wine-red Jaguar. It had to be Charlie Abram's for the driver's window was down and as we moved closer we could see the key in the ignition. The clincher was a foot wide scrape from front to rear wing, on the nearside.

'Maybe I should chuck his keys in the cut,' said Blum.

I touched the scrape, appalled at Abram's carelessness, 'How can he do it to a car like this?'

'More blummin' money than sense, 'Blum said, 'One day he'll kill himself -- or some other poor sod.'

He moved to the front wall of the pub and stepped up on to the bench under the window. He peered over the frosted glass section bearing the etched words *Walker's Warrington Ales*, then jumped down.

'They're just standing there supping like blummin' machines, ignoring each other,' he said, 'Let's get 'em at each other's throats again, eh?'

'What for?'

'Why not?'

'Yeah, but all that, it was years ago.'

Blum was firm, 'I know, but nowt's happened after thirty-odd blummin' years. It's daft. We need a winner!'

I laughed. I could see he was itching to liven up a week of hum-drum spud-picking. 'Oh, yeah? How?'

Blum grinned and stepped toward Harry's Chariot. He scooped up an armful of bruised King Edwards and, checking around for any watcher, sauntered back to the new Jag. With a final check for witnesses, he took a spud and jammed it into the exhaust pipe. The moment it was out of sight, he forced in another, then another. I brought more potatoes as Blum worked fast. Ten pounds of spuds must have gone up that pipe.

Blum shoved a final potato into the chromium-plated tube, 'If that doesn't seize the bugger, nowt will!'

I was still confused; I knew little of cars and engines, 'What?'

Blum tutted and stood, 'The engine'll die on him, it'll jam up. Let's go over the bridge and watch.'

'We can't,' I said, 'We've got to get back.'

Blum blew out in frustration. He pondered. Then his eyes were darting everywhere. His hand strayed to his head, fingers feeling and drumming. He dropped to his knees and peered under Harry Catlow's trailer. He turned and smiled.

'We don't have to be back 'til old Harry is.'

'It doesn't mean Charlie'll be out before Harry.'

Blum considered a moment, 'Dun't matter, I suppose. All we need to know is the Jag'll seize up. I reckon old Harry'll get the blame and all.'

'I don't get this...'

Blum cut me off. 'I just need to try something now we've got things moving. Just watch me and do what I do.'

Blum crawled under the trailer. Its base boards were about three foot above the ground. Underneath were two bulky axles. Blum swung a leg over the front axle and pulled himself up and on to the flat cover over the shaft. I scrambled underneath to join him, but he hissed, 'Not this one, the back one!'

I crabbed over and followed his example on the rear axle. He gave me the thumbs up.

The penny dropped. I couldn't hide my alarm, 'You mean we're going back to the field like this? -- With that mad bastard driving?'

His finger went to his lips and he grinned, 'Ssh! '

We waited. I dreaded a return to the spud field clinging under Harry's trailer, but tried to follow Blum's example of patient observation. Our field of view was small, only a few square yards of cobbles on the pub forecourt. The door of the pub opened and closed a few times in ten minutes, but all I could see were legs walking away towards the swing bridge. Then a pair of feet and legs dressed in brogue shoes and tweed trousers came into sight. Their progress across my field of view was unsteady. It had to be Charlie Abram -- Harry Catlow always wore wellies.

I focused on the feet and swaying legs and saw the edge of the Jag's door as it was opened. Charlie Abram flopped into the seat and closed the door.

Blum whispered, 'Ha, I didn't think he'd be out this soon. This'll be good!'

A few moments later, we heard the engine turn over. A grind of gears followed as he put the Jag into reverse. Abram revved hard to reverse up the slope from the pub. Then the engine faltered. He revved harder. The engine was in obvious distress, but still he revved and revved again. There was a shuddering noise and it stopped. Then came a gush of blasphemy and swear words about his latest purchase. Had the directors of Jaguar motors heard him, their ears would have glowed for a fortnight.

We struggled to contain our laughter. But it stopped the moment the taproom door opened and closed and a pair of dirty wellies came into sight. Abram was still cursing, but there was no comment from Harry Catlow as the wellies came to a halt. All we heard was a full throated hawking as the man in the wellies summoned up all his contempt and spat. I saw the obscene result hit the ground by the Jag door. Then my baulk of disgust turned to fear as the wellies went out of sight.

Harry Catlow gunned the Chariot's engine, Blum hissed, 'Hold tight!'

What followed were four or five minutes of terror. Worse than any form of transport in any set of conditions I've ever experienced. The ground seemed to race past at a hundred miles an hour. Each bump jolted the breath from my lungs. Every second I was convinced we would be thrown off into the blur of tarmac and dragged along it, flesh torn from our bones, as though the lane were a massive, running belt of super-rough sandpaper. When the Chariot reached the spud field the speed reduced, but the jolting increased. By the time the trailer halted, I felt like I'd been rolled down Ben Nevis in a dolly tub.

'Quick! Off!' Blum gasped. We managed to drop from the axles seconds before the trailer moved off. With shaking legs, I grabbed a hamper. With everyone trying to look busy in front of the boss, we didn't attract any attention as, heads down, we started to pick spuds.

Blum said, 'Better than owt you get at Blackpool fair.'

*

NEXT MORNING I ached all over as we endured another four hours' toil in the spud field. Dinnertime approached and Blum announced we'd be back on the axles. I protested, 'What for? Are you mad?'

'We haven't finished yet.' said Blum

'Finished what?'

The Chariot was crawling towards us. I looked and saw Harry Catlow tip the last of his rum down his throat. As he lowered the empty flask, he spotted us inactive. He shouted, jabbing his flask towards us, 'Did I say it were dinnertime? Get back ter work.'

We stooped to our work. Blum said, 'I thought you wanted to find out what their fight was about?'

'I do, yeah, but…'

'This is our only way. I want them screaming for blood and I'm going to blummin' do it.'

He looked up the field at the retreating trailer.

'Next time he passes, we'll tip our hampers, move behind and jump on.'

I trusted Blum's plan, but I was still reluctant about a Chariot ride, 'Do we have to?'

'We can't take the risk of being seen on the lane. It's got to look like we never left this blummin' field.'

The thought of repeating the nightmare ride made my legs shake. The minutes passed and my nervousness increased. Harry Catlow and his trailer turned back down the field. As I continued to pick spuds I kept one eye on the tractor, hoping he would turn off course, drive hell for leather to the pub before he reached us.

Blum called over, 'What time is it?'

I pushed my sleeve back and checked my Timex. 'Just gone ten to twelve.'

'Nah, I mean exactly.'

I checked again. It was eight minutes to the hour.

Blum was keyed up, 'Get ready, we've got three minutes.'

I watched as the tractor and trailer turned again and Harry Catlow started on his way back up towards us at less than walking speed.

'I'll get on the front axle,' Blum said.

The tractor and trailer edged closer and closer. I tightened my grip on my hamper. As the tractor passed, Blum moved forward and lifted and tipped his part-full hamper over the side of the trailer. He cast the hamper aside and ducked under the trailer. I did the same and let my hamper tumble as I scooted behind and underneath. The trailer moved slowly, but I had to crouch and move forward to keep up. I grabbed the ledge over the axle and pulled myself up. I nearly fell off as my head banged on the boards above me. It hurt like mad, but I couldn't let go to rub it. Seconds later I was glad I kept tight hold as the trailer lurched to the right and the tuk, tuk, tuk of the Chariot's engine increased its tempo.

Blum whooped, 'You'd have to pay for this on the fairground!'

That journey was the same nightmare in reverse. But for some reason, the nightmare didn't seem to last as long. By the time we reached the pub I'd mastered the knack of closing my eyes and gripping the axle housing with hands, elbows and knees. The Fordson's engine stopped and I saw the dirty wellies hit the cobbles and stride for the door.

I was about to get down when I heard the sound of another tractor. 'Don't move,' said Blum.

We lay still. I saw the brogues and tweed trousers of Charlie Abram climb down into view. Above the sound of this latest tractor came the shout of Abram's eldest son, 'Don't expect me to come and fetch yer!'

The wine-red Jaguar wasn't there and Charlie Abram had hitched a tractor ride.

Abram shouted back, 'Just get our Christopher to bring the Jag back 'ere from the mechanic's.'

Abram's legs moved towards the pub door and the tractor reversed and sped away.

We climbed down, but squatted under the trailer, peering out, and alert for anyone who might see us. All was quiet; until we heard a raised and angry voice from inside the pub. We swapped a look.

Blum grinned, 'Aye, aye, I wonder if that's Charlie Abram?'

I followed him as he sneaked to the bench by the window. We stood on the bench and peered in over the frosted lower section. Harry Catlow stood still, his eyes straight ahead; his only movement the steady tipping and swallowing of his pint. Charlie Abram stood across from him, waving his arm, jabbing a finger towards him, berating him. Fat Cyril Edensor, the landlord, his mouth hanging open, newspaper forgotten, stared at Abram in morbid fascination; I wondered if he'd ever heard Abram speak so much. Harry Catlow didn't react, let Charlie Abram's rant flow over and past him.

Blum whispered, 'I guessed Catlow might ignore him, but we can't have that.'

He clapped me on the shoulder. 'Right, get on the tractor. Quick!' I watched as he stepped down and moved to Harry's Chariot and clambered up on to the seat.

I swung myself up on to the wide mudguard as Blum clicked on the Fordson's magneto switch. He stamped the accelerator as the engine caught and waggled the gear shift into place. Blum might have been only fifteen, but I had no worries about him taking control of a tractor. His Uncle Walter had a reputation for fettling tractors and had taught Blum how to drive one.

Blum hauled the tractor and trailer round and off the cobbled forecourt. It was crucial when Harry Catlow heard the Chariot fire up and came out to investigate, he couldn't see who was driving. The trailer lurched on to the road and Blum accelerated. As we headed for the corner of the lane, Blum yelled, 'Has he come out?'

I had to stand and twist around to peer back past the swaying trailer. A hundred yards behind us I saw Harry Catlow run into the lane waving his arms, his army great coat flapping around his wellington boots. It was obvious he was shouting, but the noise of the Chariot and the clanking trailer blotted out all hope of hearing him.

Blum was anxious we weren't seen. He increased speed, slowing only as we reached a track on the right. It wasn't the main approach to Abram's farm, but led the back way to its barns and outbuildings. Blum had planned that our arrival on Abram land coincided with the two Abram sons and any hired men being inside for dinner. The trailer wobbled as we turned left and headed towards the farm.

Two hundred yards on, Blum slewed the tractor and trailer to a stop between the long hump of a beetroot clamp and a corrugated iron Dutch barn. He switched off the tractor engine and looked out across the field. Through a gap in the trees along the lane, it would be possible to see the Chariot and its trailer full of spuds outlined against the end of the high barn.

Blum's knowledge of the lay of the land in the parish always impressed me. Without a word, he beckoned me to follow him across the end of Abram's yard and we scurried to a thicket of scrub willow, alder and elder trees. A wall of dry grass, dead willow herb and nettles was head high. We crashed into this jungle, having to avoid old cabbage boxes, scrap iron and all the other discarded detritus of a farm. At first it seemed pointless to run into the thicket, but it was situated on a meander of the wide stream that ran the length of the parish. Twenty yards into the thicket we saw the sandy banks covered in summer's now dead vegetation. We scrambled down eight feet until we stood in the bed of the stream.

After a warm summer and no recent heavy rain, the water was down to a trickle and we were able to hurry along the stream bed, skirting or jumping the deeper pools, all the time invisible, as we headed back towards the lane. When we reached the lane, we could see the culvert which carried the stream under the roadway. We bent double and ducked inside, the swish of our wellies and heavy breaths echoing inside the brick tunnel.

Once out in daylight, the watercourse meandered across Abram's, then Catlow's land. It would have been quicker to cut across the fields between us and the spud-picking venue, but Blum was adamant we had to get back unseen; it wouldn't suit his plan for us to be connected in any way with the missing tractor and trailer load of King Eddies.

We followed the bed of the stream, beneath the level of the flat fields, startling snipe, moorhens and a couple of water voles, who sat up to peer at the unfamiliar invaders before vanishing into their bank side burrows. Our only problems were the distance we had to cover owing to the stream's wandering route -- and several barbed wire fences which crossed the stream. The wire was hung with thorn bushes, tree branches, split straw bales and other flotsam washed downstream after last winter's storms.

It was almost one o'clock when we reached the end of the spud field. We climbed up the sandy bank and peered across the churned up rudges dotted with hampers. A group of kids were hurling potatoes at each other. Others were packing away after their outdoor meal; older pickers stamped their feet against the cold and lit up a last fag before work resumed. We scrambled out of hiding and mooched our way up the field to join the fag smokers.

We listened in to the idle conversation. Soon, the other workers realised Harry Catlow was late back. Speculation about his drinking and the possibility he'd crashed his Chariot ran around the group. Blum caught my eye and nodded across to Harry Catlow's hired man. He was engaged in conversation with the Missus. The full-timer moved to his tractor and un-coupled the spinner. Mrs Catlow climbed aboard, then he joined her and they drove off the field.

We spent the next hour or so idling and smoking while we waited for our boss's return. Most of the workforce was ready to call it a day when we saw Harry Catlow driving the Chariot and empty trailer across the spud field towards us. Behind him came his full-timer on the other tractor.

I looked at Blum, 'What do you reckon's happened?'

He shrugged, 'Nowt.'

'You mean all that was a waste of time?'

'Nah, I mean nowt's happened yet.'

Catlow's voice roared across the field to the workforce, 'Don't stand bloody gawping. Back to work, the lot 'o thee!'

We hefted a hamper each.

'Doesn't sound too happy, does he?' grinned Blum, 'Can't wait 'til opening time.'

ALL AFTERNOON HARRY Catlow was in a temper. He sacked two boys from the seat of his moving Chariot for no discernible reason. They stared at him, mouths open, until a blast of four-letter rage swept them from the field. We kept our heads down as he shouted various abusive remarks at the pickers' slowness, failure to collect all the exposed King Edwards, or simply to get out of the bloody way.

There was no usual shout from him to pack up as the light began to fade and he kept us all at work until we struggled even to see any spuds, never mind pick them. Back at the yard, the Missus paid out the day's wages by the light of a paraffin lantern. As a rule, Harry Catlow hovered in the background at these times in case of disputes, but this evening he was away up the lane in the Fordson. His wife watched him go as she counted out my handful of half-crowns. Blum was anxious to leave and all but snatched his wages from the Missus' hand. He set a fast pace as we clumped up the lane in our wellie boots.

'Reckon we should nip in the Plough Horse and get a bag of crisps apiece,' he said.

I caught the grin of anticipation on his face as we passed the first road lamp outside the house called Windhover. But there was no need to check progress inside the pub. The action had already spilled out of the front door. When we rounded the bend in the lane I could see the bulk of Cyril Edensor standing in the doorway of the pub. The Chariot and the apparently repaired red Jag were parked up side by side. Fat Cyril was trying to keep the peace, but Harry Catlow and Charlie Abram ignored his bleating calls for calm and his flailing arms. Harry Catlow pushed Charlie Abram in the chest. Abram stood firm and returned the push.

We moved closer to the hedge as we neared the cobbled forecourt and crept to the gateway into the pub yard.

'Who else had spuds? Who else'd stick them up my exhaust pipe?' shouted Abram, 'Cost me damn near three hundred quid to get that engine right.'

'I never touched your bloody car -- you just thought I did,' said Catlow, poking Abram in the chest, 'So thee had them bloody sons of yours come and steal my trailer load o' praters! Dozy buggers weren't even clever enough to hide 'em!'

'My lads had nowt to do with your spuds,' Abram shouted, 'You arranged all this to make it look bad for me. Not content with damn near ruining a brand new car. Do you think I'm daft?'

The pushing and shoving and allegation and counter allegation went on for a minute or two.

'It were nowt to bloody do wi' me,' shouted Abram.

Catlow came straight back, 'That's what tha said the last bloody time.'

Abram was indignant, 'You what?'

Blum and I swapped a look. I was about to speak, but Blum put his finger to his lips and nodded towards the rowing farmers.

Catlow was now frustrated, 'Don't act the bloody goat with me. Tha know what I'm talking about.'

Abram was incensed. He pushed Catlow square in the chest, 'I'm no thief. I never touched your pint.'

Catlow pushed him back, equally hard. His face was flushed in anger, 'Now you're a liar *and* a thief. Again! Thee have been all tha bloody life.'

Abram's blood was pumping , 'You knew it'd gone the hour and you'd supped up and forgot the last orders, so you thought you'd get my pint off me with your fibbing. I never drank your pint.'

'Liar!' shouted Harry Catlow.

Charlie Abram stepped forward, 'Nay, it's you that's the liar and you that's the thief. You took my pint and got it down your neck knowing I'd ordered and paid for it.'

Catlow spat back, 'Oh, no, I didn't. I paid for that bloody pot of ale and it were mine. Nobody calls me a liar and a thief!'

Abram roared, 'That's what you are—a bloody liar and a bloody thief!'

'I'll have thee, yer bloody slanderin' swine!'

Harry Catlow tore off his army greatcoat. Charlie Abram dragged one arm, from his tweed jacket, shook the rest of it from his body. Catlow lunged at Abram, but Abram had his arm around Catlow's head in a flash. Catlow kidney-punched Abram and they broke apart. They circled each other. Abram landed a punch on Catlow's chin, but he rolled with it and returned a punch of equal force which caught his opponent across the side of his head. He followed it up with a punch to the chest, but Abram came straight back into the fray and they traded blow for blow.

Then a car horn blared. An Austin A40 braked in front of the two men, its head lights projecting their giant-sized shadows on the whitewashed front of the pub, locked in brawling combat, like grotesque shadow theatre. The doors of the Austin flew open and the wives of Catlow and Abram stepped out.

'What in God's name do you think you're doing?' shouted Mrs Abram.

'You stop that now Harry Catlow or so help me I'll have the police out to you!' Mrs Catlow screeched.

The two men stepped apart, breathing hard.

'He bloody started it,' said Harry Catlow.

'Lying again!' said Abram.

'Charlie, stop this, now!' said Mrs Abram.

'He's lying, like he's lied all his life!' said Charlie Abram. Catlow swung a punch, but his wife pushed him and he staggered, almost losing his balance. Abram took the opportunity and went to finish the job, but his missus caught at his arm, spoiling the swing.

'He stole my bloody pint!' bellowed Harry Catlow.

Charlie Abram jabbed his finger at the other man, roaring, 'Listen to him! Listen to his lies!'

'I thought this was about the car?' said Mrs Abram.

'I thought it was about the praters?' said Mrs Catlow.

Charlie Abram screeched, 'Why do you think he tried to bugger up my car?'

Harry Catlow bellowed back, 'He still won't admit he stole my pint!'

'What's this? When?' said Mrs Catlow.

'In nineteen thirty!' Catlow bawled.

'It were nineteen twenty nine!' said Charlie Abram.

'It were nineteen bloody thirty!' said Harry Catlow.

'God in Heaven, you're like a pair of kids,' said Mrs Catlow. She pointed at her husband, 'Get on that tractor and get yourself home, you wazzock.'

'You can do the same and all, Charlie Abram,' said his wife, 'In that car now.'

Charlie Abram protested, 'Not 'til he admits it were my pint.'

Catlow screeched, 'It were bloody mine! It's time for thee to admit it!'

'Over my dead bloody body,' said Charlie Abram.

'Now!' shouted their wives in unison.

Both men picked up their coats and glared at each other as they put them on. Both wives watched, their arms folded, as their still seething men prepared to go home. We withdrew into the shadows of the gateway.

'Now you know, eh?' said Blum, much amused, 'All them years, all that, over a pint of blummin' ale.'

*

NEXT DAY THE Jag and the Chariot were parked up outside the Plough Horse on the stroke of noon. That dinnertime we went in to buy some crisps from Cyril Edensor who pushed his *Daily Sketch* aside while he served us. In the taproom Harry Catlow supped at his pint as he stared into fresh air. In the parlour Charlie Abram stared into another part of the small space between them while siphoning down his own ale.

Blum had livened up our spud-picking, but between the two farmers nothing had changed. For the rest of their lives, they never again exchanged a single word, according to Fat Cyril when I reminisced with him in his retirement.

When the breathalyser came in a few years later Charlie Abram was banned from driving on two occasions. The magistrates told him if it happened again he would go to prison. His family persuaded him to stop driving for good and until his death in his eighties he walked everywhere and even gave up on his career as a drinker.

Harry Catlow continued to drive to the pub three times a day and never had occasion to blow in the bag. He died at the age of seventy one after closing time one night in the hot summer of 1976 when he had a heart attack at the wheel of his tractor driving back from the Plough Horse. It smashed the gates of the house called Windhover. Poor Harry Catlow broke his neck before the cardiac arrest could finish him. The post mortem report at the inquest revealed old Harry had drunk that sweltering day the equivalent of twenty-five pints of bitter.

I suppose nobody will ever know who was telling the truth about that single pint one night, now more than eighty years ago. Or even if its supposed theft was no more than the imagination of two drunkards. Nevertheless, without Blum's determined curiosity, nobody would've discovered the real reason for that long, silent feud.

The Home Secretary's Last Drive

WHEN WE SLOGGED into the cobbled yard at Home Farm at tea-time on the last day of August, Blum was intrigued to see two police panda cars parked up by the midden and three constables and their sergeant searching the outbuildings.

Blum checked his pace to look, 'Aye, aye. Wonder what they're up to? Someone must've pinched summat.'

'They can rob the whole estate, as far as I'm concerned,' I said, not missing a step. My eyes were on the path out of the yard that led to the wood and the head keeper's house. All I wanted was to sit down with a pint of Blum's mam's cousin Marion's home-brewed ginger beer.

Viv was of the same mind. She'd heard me going on about Marion's hot weather tonic for the past two hours and was now a follower in my quest. After a few moments, we looked back with impatience and saw Blum linger a moment before a meaningful look from the police sergeant spurred him to flick his fag end on to the midden and move along.

Blum hurried to catch us up. He was still curious about the coppers. 'Wonder what they're looking for?'

Viv laughed, 'You want to watch they don't see that Guinness bottle label where your tax disc should be.'

I laughed, 'I missed that -- A Guinness label?'

Blum was unconcerned,' Ha, I've put a note under it to say it's in the post.'

Viv rolled her eyes, 'That'll be fine then.'

Blum laughed and put his arms around our shoulders, 'Right, I could blummin' murder a pint of our Marion's ginger beer. What about you two?'

Viv elbowed his ribs. 'Listen to him. Why do you think we're in such a hurry?'

He laughed and kissed her on the cheek. He'd confided to me last time we went drinking that he was smitten with Viv. Of all places, he'd met her in a scrap yard when she helped him find some piece or other for his renovated Chevrolet. She was looking for a part for her motorbike. When she knocked the scrappie's price down for him, he invited her for a drink. When Blum discovered her dad owned a garage just a couple of miles from May Bank View, that she drove cars as well as a motorbike, enjoyed fishing, knew more about engines than he did and could split a playing card side-on with an air-rifle, he knew she was worth asking out again. I liked her and we got along well.

Since ten o'clock that morning, the three of us and some of the estate's regular beaters had moved through acre after acre of stubble, spud, carrot and sugar beet fields 'blanking-in' for the opening of the partridge shooting season, which by statute and tradition starts on the first day of September. It was common practice in the hey-day of driven partridge shooting to' blank-in' or concentrate the coveys, or family groups of the plump little game birds, into one section of farmland to provide the line of guns with a consistent flow of birds flying over them. Usually, they were walked and flushed into an area of ground with plenty of cover like a big root field. To do so took time and a lot of walking.

I'd agreed to beat on the opening day and planned to finish an overdue sixth-form essay before doing so. But Marion's husband, Ted, the head keeper, found himself short-handed for the blanking-in and Blum's mam volunteered her only son. In turn, he volunteered Viv. I'd just settled to continue with my essay when they arrived at our house to press gang me.

Blum airily dismissed my reluctance to abandon my dissertation on the *Merchant of Venice*. 'Look out the blummin' window ,'he said, 'Are you telling me old Shakespeare would've carried on scribbling if he had the chance to be out in the fields on a crackin' day like this?'

He had a point. It was a perfect end-of- summer day. Five minutes later I was in the back seat of Blum's turquoise Chev, as we drove across the flat moss land and the parish boundary to the Tarlscough estate's head keeper's house.

Ted Crossman's family had been gamekeepers on Tarlscough for generations. Ted's father, Bill, kept his job when the estate changed hands in the late'40s after the death of old Lord Tarlscough. His heir, the new Lord Tarlscough, sold up to pay death duties. He spent what was left chasing film starlets around Europe and would later drink himself to death on the island of Ischia. When old Bill died,

Ted continued as head keeper for the new owner, industrialist Sir Reuben Leggat, who died in 1960.

Ted's current boss was Julian Leggat, the son of Sir Reuben. Once the Leggats ran a machine tools business in Lancashire, but, looking ahead, Reuben had diversified into manufacturing components for cars, vans, buses and lorries. When Julian Leggat took over his father's empire, he made the venture even more of a success and it became a company vital to Britain's motor industry. He invested more of the family wealth into the estate than his father ever did. While Sir Reuben was content to play the squire and skimp on the estate's budget like the Tarlscoughs before him, Julian set out to update the estate's tenant farms. Even the tied cottages were renovated and provided with modern sanitation, as was the head keeper's house on the edge of a birch wood behind Home Farm's rambling outbuildings.

We trudged up the cart track to the Crossmans' house as Ted returned in his Ford van with his dogs. He pulled up alongside the quarter-acre of wire-netting pheasant-rearing pens. Ted called as he put the dogs in their kennels, 'Thanks for today, kids. Bloody good work. Still on for the morning?'

'We'll be here,' Blum said.

Ted hurried to join us.

'Grand as bloody owt,' Ted said, 'Get your-bloody-selves in the bloody kitchen for a bloody drink'

His words were drowned out by a screech. 'Stop 'em. Ted! Quick!'

Two big white hens missing most of their feathers flapped towards us at full belt squawking in panic. Each had clipped wings, so their attempts to fly were reminiscent of pioneer aircraft struggling to take off. From round the back of the house and into the passageway ran Marion in wellies and overalls streaked in hen muck, her arms flapping like the fleeing hens.

'Bloody Norah,' said Ted

Blum shouted, 'I'll take the left.'

I presumed he meant me to catch the one on the right, so I lunged that way and crashed into Viv. We both grabbed at fresh air as the hen barrelled between us and headed towards the pheasant pens. Before I could move, Viv was after the second hen like a shot. Meanwhile, Blum struggled to pinion the wings of the first hen which was almost as big as a turkey. Blum closed its beak with finger and thumb to stop its squawking.

'Christ All-bloody-mighty, what the bloody hell's going on?' said Ted, 'Where the bloody hell did them buggers bloody come from?'

Marion turned to Blum, 'Thanks, love, poor things are frittened to death.'

'Can anyone hear a bloody word I'm bloody saying?' said Ted.

Marion nodded to Viv as she ran to and fro along the wire pens, trying to trap the second flapping hen. 'Can Vivien manage?'

'She'll be fine,' said Blum.

Ted's voice was louder. 'Is everyone bloody deaf? Am I in-bloody-visible?'

'I got 'em from work, stop fussing,' Marion said.

As well as working as a team with Ted and his under-keeper, Marion topped-up the Crossmans' income working at a local battery egg unit run by one of the tenant farmers.

Ted ranted, 'Bantams, bloody quail, fancy-bloody- ducks, fantail-bloody-doves, twenty-bloody-two bloody canaries, two score o' bloody budgies, haven't we got enough bloody birds to feed without bringing in clapped-out bloody battery hens?'

Viv returned holding the hen. Her hand covered its eyes and its bulk was now settled in her arms, its clucks slow and quiet.

'Well?' Ted's frustrated shout was unnecessary now calm had returned. I could hear bees buzzing around the dusty dahlias on the path side as Marion faced him and ended the short breakout of peace.

It was her turn to reach top note, 'If it were down to me, Ted Crossman, I'd have a hundred of 'em here. These two are the lucky ones. Jim Fisher's got new'uns coming in the morning, so he's dumped the rest of 'em in Black Moor wood. Poor things. Thinks I don't know what he's up to, but I know he's left them for the foxes to see to.'

Ted roared, 'He bloody what?' His neck bulged inside his Tattersall check collar. To him a fox on his patch was the equivalent of raising the Devil.

'He's letting the foxes kill them?' said Viv, 'That's horrible.'

'What he's bloody doing is feeding bloody vermin,' said Ted, 'Haven't I got enough bloody problems with tomorrow and that pompous little bastard politician inviting his-bloody-self for the opening bloody day without...?'

We swapped a quick look between us. What was Ted on about?

But Marion knew, 'Not him?'

'Aye, that bloody fat-arsed little twat masquerading as the Home- bloody- Secretary, the jumped-up bloody...'

Marion was torn between anger and embarrassment in Viv's presence. 'Ted! Not in front of...'

But Blum and I were amused to see Viv struggle to stop a fit of the giggles. Ted caught her stifled merriment

'It's nowt to bloody laugh about.' Then, to Marion, 'The bloody boss wants me to bloody load for the bastard and all. I despise the short-arsed, bloody gobshite. Greediest bloody shot I've ever seen. Thinks every bloody bird in the bloody drive is his and no one bloody else's.'

Marion was straight in. 'Then tell the boss you won't.'

Ted was loud in his frustration, 'How the bloody hell can I do that? What can I bloody do when a bloody cabinet minister keeps inviting his-bloody-self when he bloody feels like it just 'cause the boss's old man asked him to shoot here once or bloody twice?'

'You can tell Julian Leggat the shoot's off if he lets that excuse for a man on here with a gun in his hands,' said Marion, 'Cabinet Minister, or not.'

'It's not my bloody place to bloody tell him.'

'You told me last time he was here that the boss as much as said he weren't wanted. And that was before what happened.'

Ted floundered, 'Bloody…Christ…You know…You bloody know I bloody can't, love.'

Marion was firm. 'If he's coming you can do without me on the beating line tomorrow.'

Ted's collar and tie were choking him, his face bright red, 'You bloody what?'

Marion ignored him and signalled us to follow her with the rescued battery hens.

She turned back to Ted, 'And you've got another think coming if you imagine I'm serving up my best shoot-day hot-pot for the Guns and beaters. Not with him there. He made it quite clear what he thought of it last time.'

'Marion, love,' said Ted.

But she ignored him as she ushered us up the side of the house. The three of us were desperate for details we didn't know.

'Bloody hell,' said Ted.

*

IN THE BIG, untidy kitchen, Marion served up our long-awaited pints of ginger beer as Ted came in to plead for her co-operation the next day. He tried every approach he could dredge up, even suggesting Julian Leggat would be so put out by her boycott of his VIP guest that Ted would be sacked and they would be evicted from the head keeper's house.

'Fiddlesticks, 'said Marion.

'Just you bloody wait and bloody see.'

From Marion's asides to us three as the couple bickered, it became clear why police men were searching the farm buildings. It was a security check before the arrival of the Home Secretary. Marion told us the same procedure had taken place two years before when he last came to the opening day partridge shoot at Tarlscough.

On that day the Home Secretary had made a disparaging comment on Marion's Lancashire hot-pot, comparing it to posher shoot lunches in his experience, and using the term 'peasant food.' Marion overheard his remark. Even members of the aristocracy had in the past complimented her on her hot-pot. Without a thought for her position, she rounded on the Home Secretary and reminded the whole company of shooters and beaters of the Right Honourable minister's origins in the terraced streets of Leyland and his previous job as a bus works labourer.

Marion pointed her ladle at the cabinet minister, 'I wonder if your voters who eat hot-pot to make ends meet know you think they're peasants.'

She turned her back on the red-faced politician, surprised and relieved Julian Leggat appeared to turn a blind eye to the Home Secretary's embarrassment and a deaf ear to the resultant merriment of his other guests.

'Not that I was that bothered,' she told us, 'I wouldn't take a snide remark from the Duke of Edinburgh, never mind that twerp.'

'It were only bloody words,' said Ted,' Everyone knows he's a jumped-up bloody trade unionist who went for the good life the bloody minute he walked into the House of bloody Commons. Little arse-hole sold out his own bloody supporters without a bloody…'

Marion cut him off. 'What about young Luke Markland?'

Ted fell silent, but Marion told us. 'Home Secretary or not, he's a dangerous Shot. Any shooter with an ounce of sense knows not to shoot forward on partridges when the beaters are in sight. But, no, that didn't apply to the Home Secretary, did it? He lets off two shots – not a bird touched -- and Luke gets good and peppered.'

'He shot him?' said Viv.

'I dug three pellets out of his face,' said Marion, 'The hospital did the others. Poor lad were lucky he weren't blinded.'

She nodded to Ted. 'I've seen that husband of mine pull the gun out of a dangerous Shot's hands and curse him all the way back to his car, pack him off home his ears ringing with curses. But not that time, oh, no, not to a special VIP guest of the boss.'

Ted chewed at his lip in embarrassment.

Marion went on, 'Most shooters would've been at the lad's side to apologise. Most would've given him at least a week's wage on the spot and told everyone they were leaving the shoot that minute. Not him. He were laughing and bragging and being his objectionable self the rest of the day like nowt happened – and not a penny offered to see young Luke right. My husband there knew what he'd done, but it didn't stop him accepting a ten pound note off him at the end of the day.'

Ted blushed and made a lame attempt to redeem the situation, 'Aye, I know all that, but I'll be loading his bloody guns for him this time. I'll be there for every bloody shot and it won't bloody happen again. Not bloody likely.'

'You can do what you like,' Marion said, 'But I'm having nowt to do with it. I don't want owt to do with anyone else getting hurt, or worse.'

She turned her back on him and went out to feed her poultry. A desperate Ted hurried after her.

*

A SHORT TIME later, a subdued Ted paid us up for our day's work and reminded us of the meet up the following morning. We were about to leave when Neville, the under-keeper, arrived carrying six boxes of shotgun cartridges.

The young Scouser approached Ted. 'Gorrem, boss. Where do you want me to purrem?'

'If it were down to me I'd shove them up the pompous little bastard's ar…' He stopped, perhaps thinking better of slating a VIP guest in front of his subordinate. 'Just stick 'em in the bloody shed.'

Blum took a box from Neville's arms, 'Who's shooting a twenty-eight bore?'

Ted forgot about Neville's presence, 'Three bloody guesses,' said Ted. 'And he has the brass bloody neck to ask the Estate to bloody buy them in for him, as if he's on his bloody uppers, the tight-arsed little get. If I had my way he'd be using a bloody pea shooter.'

Blum laughed. 'Most shootin' men call twenty-eight bores blummin' pea shooters, don't they?'

'Them as can't shoot 'em, maybe. In the right hands they'll shoot as hard and straight as any bloody twelve-bore, even if there's nowt but a bloody thimbleful of bloody shot in the bloody cartridge.'

Blum looked at the load details printed on the cardboard box, 'He must be a good shot, this Home Secretary.'

'Him?! Little bastard can't bloody shoot for bloody toffee,' said Ted, 'He's got a matched bloody pair of Holland and bloody Holland twenty-eights. Bloody beautiful guns, but he's only bloody aping the top shots that use them 'cause a twelve-bore's too bloody easy for them. Never mind bloody pea-shooters, he might as well use a pair of bloody matching bloody pea sticks. No bloody partridge has owt to fear off him, the bloody cross-eyed little shithouse.'

Blum handed the box back to Neville and we left Ted to his work. I noticed Blum was drumming his fingers on his head as we reached the Chev and he handed the keys to Viv. He was quiet as Viv drove. I watched him, pondering, inhaling on his fag, letting the smoke stream out through the window of the Yank car.

After a mile or two, he turned to Viv, 'I need to get the van from work. Can you drop us off?'

'Yeah…What for?'

He grinned at her, 'I'll tell you later.' Then, he winked at me and I knew he was plotting.

*

A RED BALL of a sun was dropping through the trees around the abbey ruins as we sat in the garden behind the Scottish Soldier. Blum was quiet as we drank our pints of bitter, relaxed in the heat of the day's sunshine seeping back out of the cob walls of the oldest pub in the county.

I had planned to go home to try to finish my essay, but after two pints the will to write about the works of Shakespeare had disappeared.

'Does anyone fancy going down to the Plough Horse?' I said.

Viv chipped in, 'What about the Hare and Hounds? They've got a juke box at last.'

I felt content, 'Anywhere's fine with me.'

Blum slid a Player's Cadet from his packet and lit up. 'No time,' he said,' One more jar, a bag of chips, and we have to get cracking.'

I knew something was in his head. As usual, I knew also not to ask too much. I let Viv do that.

'Get cracking on what?'

Blum grinned, 'I think something needs to be bloody done about that Home bloody Secretary. I don't like to see Ted and our Marion bloody falling out.'

I laughed, 'Too bloody right.'

Viv looked from me to Blum, to me, then back to Blum, puzzled. 'But what? –Sorry--What bloody needs to be bloody done?'

We laughed, but had I known it would be more than twenty-four hours before I got to bed again, the bitter in my belly may not have aroused as much enthusiasm.

*

THE LAST THING I felt like was a day's beating as I arrived with Blum at Home Farm yard next morning. Blum looked far from tired, though, and his eyes shone with the anticipation I'd seen so many times. Ted and Neville moved around the yard to greet the beaters and Mr. Leggat's guest Guns for the partridge shoot. The guest list was made up of relatives and friends of the owner as well as keen shooters from the estate's farm tenants. Rather than a bag of hundreds of birds, the opening day shoot was more of a day for renewing friendships and enjoying a day in the fresh air. Most guests didn't shoot and came for the day out alone.

The only faces missing belonged to Viv, Marion and the Home Secretary. Viv had gone to the head keeper's house to speak to Marion, but the Right Honourable gentleman was late. I wondered, if, after all our efforts, some political crisis had forced him to change his plans, but Julian Leggat interrupted my thoughts when he clapped his hands to call everyone to attention.

He was a tall, languid man of about thirty-five with fashionable long, blond hair. Rumour had it he once decked Mick Jagger at a party in Knightsbridge in an argument over a girlfriend. But today he looked like a classic English landowner in London-cut tweed shooting suit and brown fedora hat. He didn't shoot often, but was usually in the line of Guns on September the first. But Neville told us that the boss had last night declined an offer to have his gun checked over and told him the Home Secretary would be taking his place. Blum and I swapped a look when Neville revealed the blanked in area of land would be flushed of birds earlier than usual as the VIP guest had to be back later that day in Westminster. Blum grinned with satisfaction.

Julian Leggat welcomed the guests and announced the Home Secretary was running late, so the head keeper's customary address and the draw for pegs for the day's positions on the shooting line would go ahead while his arrival was awaited. Mr Leggat himself would draw a peg on the Home Secretary's behalf. I overheard grumbling and sarcastic comments from the Guns, most of it from the invited farmers; all of them small 'c' and big 'C' conservatives to a man.

Ted finished his almost expletive-free speech on safety and the day's 'batting order' when a police man on a maroon Velocette motorbike led a big black car into the yard. We watched as a chauffeur got out and opened the rear door. The Home Secretary's personal detective slipped from the other side of the car and watched, incongruous in his blue lounge suit, as his minister stepped out, all five feet nothing of him, dressed to the nines in expensive-looking shooting clobber.

Julian Leggat strolled to the car to greet his guest, flanked by Ted in his best tweed Norfolk jacket and plus two breeks. Over Ted's shoulder was a leather bag containing the Home Secretary's twenty-eight bore cartridges. Ted couldn't hide his scowl as Leggat welcomed the cabinet minister and the politician's chauffeur dumped a double gun case in Ted's arms.

Blum was bubbling in anticipation of the day, in high spirits, 'Get a load of Ted's face. Talk about licking shite off a blummin' thistle.'

I laughed as I heard the Home Secretary's high-pitched voice with its trace of a north-west accent. 'Always a pleasure to be invited to Tarlscough for the first day, Julian. Best partridge drives in the north of England.'

We were unable to hear more as Neville urged us beaters towards the tractor and trailer to take us out to the fields. We climbed aboard and crushed together, sitting on straw bales. As the tractor moved off, I heard a shout and saw Marion and Viv running after the trailer.

Marion shouted, 'Whoa! Hang on! Not so fast!'

The tractor slowed and helping hands shot out to haul the two latecomers on board. A burly beater stood up and gave Marion his bale seat. Viv gave Blum and me the thumbs up. Owing to the crush, we were unable to talk to either Viv or Marion. I was so tired I almost fell asleep despite the bumping, lurching ride. But Blum nudged me in the ribs and pointed out a stocky bloke of about twenty with the ruddy face of a farm worker; except his left cheek bore five streaks of scar tissue, one half an inch under his eye. I looked at Blum, a question, and he nodded confirmation. It was Luke Markland.

The tractor pulled up and Neville directed the beaters to line out the length of a spud field about

300 yards wide. While Neville gave final instructions, Julian Leggat's Land Rover passed. I glimpsed the Home Secretary in the passenger seat. He didn't look our way and his face bore a fixed, supercilious smile. I couldn't see if he had cross eyes. On the back of the Landy were Ted and the uncomfortable minister's detective. Ted spotted Marion and his face lit up.

'You're bloody here,'he shouted. Marion blew him a kiss. 'What about the bloody hot-pot? Is it bloody…?' But his words were lost as the Landy bounced along the rutted track.

On one end of the line Neville was 'flanker.' He and his opposite number on the other end each carried coloured canvas flags that snapped and crackled if shaken and waved. The purpose of the flags was to stop partridges from flying 'out of the side' instead of over the guns. By judicious movement the flag could push the coveys over the guns. Neville was about to blow his whistle to get the line moving on the half-mile push to the shooting line when Blum buttonholed him.

'Uncle Ted said I could go on the flank today,' he said, 'So I can show my mate here how it's done.'

This was news to me. And to Neville, but he handed over his flag. 'Just be sure you gerra shed load over Lord Muck, eh?'

Blum said, 'We'll do that all right.'

He winked at me as we moved off, me taking a position about fifty yards from Blum. Neville blew his whistle and the line started to move over the now dying stalks of the spud field and the raised rudges that made progress slow and hard going.

An alert Blum was moving ahead of the line, his flag motionless in the air. I was so knackered I stumbled my way forward. I thought back to the night before. While Blum crept back to the head keeper's house Viv and me drove two miles to the edge of the estate.

Our mission took three hours of frantic work, but we managed. Meanwhile, Blum was also busy all night before stealing back to Ted's house as the first of Marion's bantam cocks crowed at the rising sun. My work with Viv was not completed until dawn either, as we dragged sack after sack across this same vast spud field and into the adjoining thirty acres of sugar beet.

The first report of a gun brought me back from my thoughts. Another shot followed, but two partridge flushed by us beaters flew unscathed over the head of a tall shooter on our end of the line of Guns. As the beating line entered the sugar beet, coveys and single birds started to flush. More shots cracked. Several birds fell, but I could see the Home Secretary had still not had a shot. He stood with his gun ready. To his side, Ted stood with the minister's second, loaded shotgun, ready to hand to him when needed.

Just then, Blum started to run. He lolloped across in front of me, then the next man on the line. I knew enough about beating to know this wasn't the right thing to do. As I slackened my step, then stopped to watch, a wave of partridges took flight; covey after covey, hundreds of birds. I could hear the sharp sound of Blum's flag as he hoisted it high, whipping and cracking it like mad. Partridges which should have flown over half the line of waiting guns were now airborne and streaking down the field, all concentrated over one Gun--the Right Honourable Home Secretary.

A shot sounded, quickly followed by another. Two more shots were fired before I saw what happened. Huge plumes of white smoke enveloped the Home Secretary. But still he fired. Later, we were told that he was still screaming for Ted to load faster as he fired shot after shot into the air, blindly poking his barrels at birds he could no longer see, as covey after covey streamed through the white clouds over his head.

I started to move forward again, quickening my pace. I could hear laughter. All eyes were on the mass of white smoke, but I remembered to look for Viv and Marion further along the line. Both of them were pulling cords from the necks of a score or more hessian spud sacks.

Nobody in the line of Guns was shooting. All were pointing and laughing at the Home Secretary, enveloped in a huge cloud of talcum powder. It must have dawned on him that something had gone wrong, for his guns became silent. A breeze whipped away the cloud of smoke. I saw him staring open-mouthed as dozens of battery hens flapped and lolloped towards him, clucking in alarm away from Viv and Marion who were almost too helpless with laughter to walk.

Through the drifting smoke I saw Julian Leggat standing smoking a cigarette with a pair of black Labradors at his heels. On his face was a smile of mild amusement. Then I saw a solemn faced Ted offer The Home Secretary a loaded gun. The minister took it and then regretted his action. In a spat of pique he thrust both guns back into Ted's arms and turned on his heel.

He pointed at Julian Leggat and shouted, 'Is this some sort of joke, Leggat?'

'Sorry?' said the languid Mr. Leggat.

Surrounded by squawking battery hens, the Home Secretary hurried on his short legs towards his bemused detective. Within a minute the detective had retrieved the minister's pair of expensive shotguns. Two minutes after that Julian Leggat was driving both of them off the field in his Land Rover. The last I saw of the Home Secretary in the flesh was his angry flushed face as he ran the gauntlet of laughing Guns, guests and beaters. Nobody was laughing, jeering and cat-calling louder than Luke Markland -- and Marion.

*

FOR THE FIRST time in living memory, the shoot lunch on September the first went on so long that no more shooting was done that day. Though it was ready later than usual, Julian Leggat himself drove out the big crock of hot-pot from Marion's kitchen to the traditional venue at a Dutch barn on one of the tenant farms. He also provided two bottles of whisky and six crates of beer; another first for opening day lunch.

Ted was at first angry at what had gone wrong. Then he demanded explanations. 'If I lose my bloody job over this there'll be bloody trouble I'm bloody telling you.'

Marion said, 'Oh, be quiet, Ted. Everyone else reckons it's the best drive they've ever had.'

He looked at me and Blum, suspicion in his eyes, 'Them bloody cartridges weren't bloody right.' Then at Marion and Viv, 'And how the bloody hell did Fisher's bloody battery hens bloody get there?'

We gave nothing away and after Mr. Leggat sought him out to congratulate him on a good morning's sport, Ted was full of conviviality. He relaxed in the late summer sun. With one arm around Marion and a huge tumbler of whisky in hand, he sat on a bale of wheat straw and declared, 'I'd made my bloody mind up today. One step out of bloody line by that pompous little bugger and I was bloody well going to send him bloody packing, Home-bloody-Secretary, or bloody not.'

Marion winked at us and linked arms with her man, 'I know you were, love.'

'Bloody right,' said Ted, 'Bloody short-arsed bloody pillock.' He snorted in his glass of whisky, much amused, 'Shooting like a madman, he was. Piss and farts coming out both barrels and he still wanted to shoot everything bloody going – even when he couldn't see! – The bloody useless little bastard!'

Lunch continued and Mr. Leggat wandered over to me, Blum and Viv as we enjoyed his beer. He eyed us in turn, 'I don't think I've seen you three beating here before...'

'I've been many a time,' said Blum, 'Ted's my mam's cousin's husband.'

'So I believe,' said Mr. Leggat, 'Your technique as a flanker was...well, different.'

Blum lowered his beer bottle and said, 'I was told to put plenty of birds over your VIP guest.'

Mr. Leggat smiled, 'Well, it seemed to work.'

There was an awkward pause. Mr. Leggat was casual with his question, 'I don't suppose any of you know anything about those rather odd cartridges the Home Secretary was shooting? Or those hens showing up on the drive?'

Viv and I cringed as Blum said, his eyes twinkling, 'Don't be blummin' daft.'

Mr. Leggat grinned, 'No, of course not. How silly of me.'

He clapped Blum on the shoulder, 'Anyway, well done. A memorable morning, indeed.' He nodded to me, then Viv, 'Thank you.'

He wandered off with his Labradors at heel. We waited a while and started to laugh.

Blum uncapped another bottle of beer, 'I don't think Ted's got owt to worry about.'

We felt we'd achieved fitting vengeance for Marion and certainly for Luke Markland.

*

OVER THE YEARS I sometimes wondered about Julian Leggat's amused acceptance of matters which could have had serious consequences for the estate's reputation, as well as Ted and Marion's job security.

Two days after the Home Secretary's last drive he was re-shuffled out of the cabinet followed by vague rumours of corruption. Ted and Marion, as well as Blum, Viv and me, were more than pleased to hear the news.

But it wasn't until the late 1990s, when the former Home Secretary was pushing up daisies after a heart attack that I read a political memoir which touched on the relationship between the erstwhile politician and Sir Reuben Leggat.

It claimed that the Labour Home Secretary, as a trade unionist, had discovered an embarrassing sexual peccadillo of Sir Reuben's then used that knowledge to secure Leggat's influence for concessions in the motor industry for his own union members. That, in turn, had secured the future cabinet minister's sponsorship for a safe Labour seat in Parliament. The memoir implied, too, that the future Home Secretary had also pocketed a substantial sum of cash to keep his knowledge to himself. All this accelerated his progress into Government and the higher end of the shooting world.

I would have liked to ask Julian Leggat about the memoir's claims, but I never met him again. I think he knew everything there was to know about the former Home Secretary. Whatever the truth of it, I do know that opening day was the last time the former Home Secretary ever went shooting and we had Blum to thank for that.

Words in the Barley

HAD I BEEN on my own, I might have slipped away before he identified me. Or perhaps suffered a good hiding had the creep recognised me before I could leg it. But the instant Cyril Clegg saw it was me with a magistrate's daughter, red-haired, red-faced, and fastening her bra, I was trapped.

Clegg stood in the open doorway. Outside, I could hear his tractor engine idling. He stepped inside the old hay store and his rat face cracked in a leering grin.

'What's been going on here, then?' he said, 'Eh, eh?'

It was obvious, but I wasn't going to cater to his sick appetite with a blow-by-blow description. Nor was Angela, who was checking she hadn't got her skirt caught up in her knickers.

I decided to face it out. I buttoned-up my best shirt and pushed it back into my waistband, 'We're just sheltering from the rain,' I said.

'Oh, aye? Rain?'

Clegg took a few steps closer. He looked at me, but his eyes were drawn to Angela as she smoothed her skirt over her legs, then pulled at strands of hay stuck in her long locks.

He gave us a twisted grin. 'I've seen no rain. Eh, eh?'

Clegg wore wellie boots, twill trousers and a tweed jacket. Most farmers round our way favoured flat caps, but Clegg wore a pork pie hat. That, and the fact he always had a clean collar and tie, rather than overalls, prompted a gut feeling he was somehow not a real farmer. He was, though. And as well as more than two hundred acres of land, this hay store belonged to him.

'It was raining when we came in, wasn't it?' I said, looking to Angela for confirmation.

She slid off the bales and stood up, making a move. 'I think we'd better go.'

Clegg took a quick step to block her path, 'Hang on, hang on.'

His voice was high-pitched for a man of around fifty and it was as if the noise came down and out of his nose, rather than his mouth.

He tore his eyes away from Angela and faced me, 'I haven't finished yet. I want to know what's been going on in my property.'

I held his eyes. 'I've told you -- nothing.'

He looked back to Angela, again with a lascivious grin, 'What would your ma and da say if they knew you'd been in here…' He hooked a thumb at me, 'with him?'

Angela avoided his eyes, looked at the ground, but didn't answer.

'What if I told them?'

Angela wouldn't look at him. Clegg reached out. He put his fingers under her chin and raised her face.

The nasal voice sounded excited, like a chattering monkey, 'What would they say? Caught in the hay with someone like him? All hot and bothered, eh? Thought about that? Have you? Eh, eh?'

I felt a surge of anger. Angela recoiled, knocked his hand away.

I stepped forward, 'Leave her alone.'

'Shut yer trap, boy.' He jabbed his fingers into my chest, 'I'm not talking to you.'

He turned back to Angela, 'Well?' he said, 'Eh, eh?'

She was scared, 'Just let us go.'

'I know who your father is.'

Angela looked at him, unsure.

'He's the Justice of the Peace, isn't he? Top dog in some bank, or other? Seen him in the Thursday *Advertiser* a time or two, eh, eh?'

Angela's face drained.

I butted in, 'You've got the wrong man.'

I regretted the remark the moment I said it. Even he seemed to notice I sounded like the baddie in a clichéd film. He gave an almost childish laugh, his shoulders bobbing up and down, sniggering.

He leered at her again, revelling in the power of his knowledge 'Lives at the Iddon's old place, white house on the cut?' Then, added with satisfaction, 'Arthur Cummings, JP. Eh, eh?'

Angela was the rabbit in the headlights. Clegg knew who she was, there was no doubt. And Arthur Cummings, JP, wasn't a founder member of the Permissive Society, even if his only daughter seemed set to be a major stakeholder.

Clegg enjoyed her discomfort in silence for a moment before he turned to me. Secretly, I was hoping he hadn't recognised me, my hair was much longer since our last run-in, but he confirmed it, 'I know plenty enough about you and all.'

Two winters ago he'd caught Blum and me shooting pheasants at roost in one of his woods. Blum pointed his stolen four-ten gun at Clegg and dazzled him with a bike lamp. In a moment of off-the-cuff insanity, Blum had put on a deep, rough Liverpudlian voice, swung the gun at him and threatened to blow his effin' brains out. Clegg backed off and we scarpered. As we fled, Clegg shouted, 'I know you -- I know your names.' Afterwards, we had visits from the police, but we'd each fixed sound, yet fictional, alibis with girls at the youth club. After a week or two of sleepless nights, the inquiry faded away.

In the memory of having escaped Clegg's push for prosecution, I found some courage. I grabbed Angela's hand and made a move, 'We've done nothing wrong so we're going.'

Clegg shifted with a shuffle, blocked our free passage. 'What about my hay bales?'

I pushed my shoulders back, playing the hard man, 'What about them?'

'I checked 'em in here myself, Tuesday. Three of 'em's been pulled open, by the look of it.'

Angela went to say something, perhaps that it was only two bales, but I got in before her. It had been her idea to pull them apart and make our chosen spot a bit more comfortable, but I wasn't going to let her admit it. Not to this creep.

'Must've been rats,' I said.

'Two-legged ones, eh, eh?'

'I wouldn't say that to the gypsies face to face,' I said, 'You don't want to get the wrong side of them, you know.'

'Don't get clever with me, boy. There's been no gyppos here.'

He held his hand out flat, waggled his fingers.

'A quid for the hay and, what say, ten bob for damages? Thirty bob, eh, eh?'

'I haven't got a penny on me,' I said.

It was the truth. I'd left two ten shilling notes and half a crown in my other jeans and couldn't even buy Angela a couple of shandies before steering her for 'a walk' down Pygon Lane.

'Just pay him and let's go,' Angela said.

'It's true, 'I said, 'I've nothing on me. Anyway, he's not getting a penny off us.'

She reached for her little, red shoulder bag. Angela didn't seem short of a few bob, maybe because Arthur Cummings, JP, was a bank's area manager, but I was damned if I was going to let her pay a brass farthing to Cyril Clegg.

I was firm. 'I said no.'

Her voice was strangled and low, as if she could prevent Clegg from hearing. She was emphatic, 'I don't want him telling my dad.'

Clegg glanced at me and then said to Angela, 'You'll have to pay me in kind, then.'

His tongue flicked across his lips Again, his shoulders quivered, it seemed, in obscene and private anticipation -- of what, I wasn't sure. But my imagination had one or two ideas and I was disgusted. Angela's hand grabbed for mine. I could tell she was as repulsed as me.

'What's that supposed to mean?' I said.

His eyes strayed to Angela again, 'You can both work off the debt.'

I came straight back at him, 'There is no debt.'

'Have it your own way then,' he said, standing aside, 'And I'll call on His Worship Mr Cummings next Sunday afternoon and tell him what I saw; tell him what his pretty daughter gets up to of an evening, eh, eh?'

'What sort of work?' Angela said.

'Don't get involved,' I snapped at her.

'Shut up!' she said. She faced Clegg. 'What work?'

'Always work to do on a farm, 'he said, 'I'll find something. If you don't want me knocking at Stopforth's Cottage come Sunday I'll see the both of you in my yard, eight sharp Saturday morning.'

'All right' Angela said.

I was appalled. 'He's bluffing.'

'I'm not bluffing, boy,' Clegg said, 'If you think I am, look out for the police at your door. Vandalism, this is. Not as bad as pointing a loaded gun, mind, but serious enough, wouldn't you say? Eh, eh?'

The loaded gun remark went over Angela's head, but I met his eyes. In them I caught the sparkle of his pleasure at some sort of personal triumph.

Angela tried to push past him, but he moved and blocked her way for a moment, before pushing her outside. I held his gaze for a few seconds more, and then followed her. I glanced back at Clegg, leaning, one arm against the hay store door post, his face a smile of sick satisfaction. I caught up with Angela.

'Dirty sod,' she said, 'He pinched my arse.'

I was furious. 'That's it, then. You've got to tell the police. It's indecent behaviour, or something. Let's get him done.'

'Are you joking? Do you want the whole world to know, never mind my dad?'

'I know, but…'

'I just want to go and get it over with.'

I looked back at Clegg watching us. I couldn't and wouldn't let him get away with this.

*

WE MET UP at Mullineux's bridge at twenty to eight on Saturday morning and followed the public footpath up past the old sand pits and about thirty acres of fresh-drilled barley to Clegg's farm. The day promised warmer sunshine than usual for late March.

The argument between Angela and me had gone on over two days. I met her once at Pilling bridge and then in the garden behind the Scottish Soldier over halves of bitter. I hated the idea of being under the thumb of Cyril Clegg. Blum and I might've done him wrong that night he caught us at the pheasants, but I couldn't stomach the idea of him achieving any sort of vengeance. Every time I thought of him and how he'd touched her sparked rushes of anger. I'd rather die, I thought, than let him get one over on me, humiliate me. I tried and tried to persuade

Angela we should ignore the Saturday appointment and call his bluff, but she wouldn't yield. Again, I suggested reporting him for indecency; again she wouldn't hear of it. Needless to say, amid all this talk, we didn't go for a walk to the hay store, or anywhere else.

When we trudged into the yard, Clegg was loading crates of swedes into the back of his Bedford van. He slammed the back doors and moved towards us, a grin on his face. Already, I could sense he was enjoying his power over us.

'Dead on time,' he said, 'I always like to see my workers punctual.'

'We're not your workers,' I said. Angela shot me a dirty look. I couldn't help it, though. Every second in his presence increased my loathing.

'You are today', he said. His eyes moved between us, 'Good to see you're fettled up for some dirty work.'

Both of us wore old clothes. Angela wore jeans and a red anorak that was too small for her ripening figure.

Clegg's eyes roved over her, 'Going to be a bit warm today. You might've done better in that pretty skirt you had on the other night.' Then added, 'Something that lets the breeze up round them long legs of yours, eh, eh?'

'Are we getting started, or what?' I said. I wanted him nowhere near Angela, or me. And every time I saw that leering grin, I wanted to drown him in his own horse trough.

Clegg nodded his head towards the end of the yard. I let Angela go first. I didn't want him walking behind her. We reached the corner by the cart shed and I saw that the yard was L-shaped. To our right it ran off at ninety degrees. It was an area of overgrown cobbles, lined by old pig sties on one side and disused stables and byres on the other.

Clegg jabbed his finger, 'See them cobbles. I don't want to see a single sod or dandelion or nettle between 'em. Scrape 'em out, rake 'em up and get 'em on the midden.'

Bloody hell. The cobbled area seemed as big as a football pitch. I swapped a look with Angela. Her dismay was equal to mine.

Clegg pointed to his right, 'There's tools and a barrer in the end sty. When I get back I want it finished.'

'When'll that be?' I said.

'Three o'clock, four o' clock. Might be earlier, might be later.'

He turned away and moved back towards the main yard.

I called after him, 'We can't finish by then.'

'You better had, boy. Or you'll see whether I'm bluffing, eh, eh?'

'Bastard,' I said, as Clegg went out of sight.

Angela headed for the pig sty and the tools as I moved to the corner of the yard. I wouldn't put it past Clegg pretending to go, and then spying on us, hoping to see more of what he walked in on at the hay store. I peered round the corner of a stable as Clegg started up the van and drove out of sight. I caught a glimpse of the van through the hedge as he turned on to the lane and drove away.

I hurried back to find Angela with a collection of rusty billhooks, a broken sickle and a pair of sheep shears.

'Come on, he's gone. We can do a bunk.'

'Don't be stupid. You heard him; he's not bluffing.'

'He is,' I insisted, 'He got what he wanted. He blackmailed us to come out here first thing of a Saturday morning. He's had his kicks.'

She faced me, 'Well, I'm doing what he says.'

'And what if he wants us to do more?' I said, 'It's true what they say about blackmailers -- they always want more. If we go now it shows him he can't piss us about.'

'You can go if you want, but I'm staying.'

'You'd risk being on your own when he comes back? He'd love that, wouldn't he?'

She picked up a billhook. 'He wouldn't dare.'

I imagined Angela chopping off Clegg's wandering hands, blood gushing on the overgrown cobbles.

She caught my eye, 'You wouldn't dare leave me on my own either.'

She was right. I wouldn't. Not with that pervert. She pressed the billhook to my chest and I took hold of it. 'Which end of the yard do you want to start?' she said.

*

FOR MOST OF the morning we worked in silence. We were too far apart to speak without the effort of shouting. The work was boring and seemed to involve the use of muscles I'd never known about. As the sun grew warmer, we made frequent trips to a tap round the corner of the yard. Neither of us had been clever enough to bring a flask, a sandwich, or even a bar of chocolate.

Angela whined that she'd skipped breakfast in her effort to be on time. Prompted by her claims of starvation, I went for a wander to see what I could forage. I found fruit trees and strawberry beds, but they offered nothing in March.

On my search I noticed that Clegg's farm was well-equipped. A new Massey Ferguson tractor stood alongside a two- year-old Ford model. His ploughs, foragers and other equipment were all new, or near to new, and so was a combine harvester draped in tarpaulin. Parked by the farmhouse was an Austin Cambridge car with last year's registration number. The house itself was freshly painted and well-kept; impressive for a bachelor farmer. After ten minutes I returned to Angela with a leek, a handful of tired purple broccoli tops and some parsley.

She regarded the lunch menu with disdain, 'Great.'

I tried to lighten our situation. 'There's some nice, nibbly chicken feed in the store.'

With a glare for me, she snatched the broccoli and flounced away to wash it under the tap. We didn't speak to each other for more than an hour.

Our silence may have been for the good. We made progress. Just after half-past-one, I wheeled back the barrow from the midden, having dumped the final load of sods and weeds. The cobbles were clear. Angela was leaning against the sandstone pig slabs, arms folded, and deep in a sulk. Before I could attempt to raise her morale, Clegg's van came around the corner and in to the transformed yard.

Clegg got out and surveyed our work for ten seconds or so, 'I knew you could do it, eh, eh?'

I refused to comment. I wouldn't show Clegg even a morsel of deference. Angela moved towards him. I cringed as she said, 'Please can we go now?'

'Have you learnt your lesson?' he said.

I cringed again as she nodded. He relished her subservience. I knew what made him tick. It was all about dominance. I hated him.

He turned to me, 'How about you, boy?'

I met his eyes, 'We're quits on the bales.'

His eyes narrowed as he nodded slowly, 'Aye, quits on the bales…'

I knew what he meant. The bales might be forgotten, but not that night in the wood. I willed myself not to look away. His eyes bored into mine. If he was looking for a confession he'd never get one. Another moment passed and he looked away, spoke to Angela:

'Off you go and we'll say no more about it.'

Angela shoved her hands in her pockets and walked away.

He called after her, 'If you fancy a nice weekend job just call at the farmhouse. Any time you like. Proper wages, eh, eh?'

But she didn't look back.

I wanted to go after her, but I forced myself to remain unhurried, casual.

With an edge of menace, the pitch of his voice lower, he said, 'Stay off my property, you little shit.'

I stared at him for a moment, trying to make him feel uneasy, then turned and strolled away as slow and dignified as I could manage.

Once around the corner, I saw Angela walking, head down, along the public footpath. I started to run. She was almost at the canal bank before I caught up with her.

'Are you all right?'

She kept walking.

'Angela?'

She didn't stop, so I caught her sleeve.

She shook my arm away, 'Don't you dare touch me.'

'What?'

She turned to me, angry.

'Do you know how…how humiliated I feel?'

'What about me?'

'I'm not talking about you! You should've let me pay him as soon as he caught us. But, oh, no, not you, you had to push it. You had to be the big man.'

I protested, 'That's not fair! If we'd done what I said and called his bluff…'

'He knows my dad. He knows where I live!'

'It's all over now.'

'Look what he's made me do!'

She thrust out her dirty, scratched hands.

'I've broken my nails, I'm filthy and I'm starving hungry. I feel like…like he's used me, the dirty, horrible creep!'

'You'll soon feel better. Get something to eat and have a bath and…'

But she buried her hands in her pockets and walked on. I followed.

'Look, how about a drink tonight?'

She stopped and faced me, 'I don't want a drink - - not with you. Not tonight, not tomorrow, not ever. We're finished.'

I stared at her in complete surprise. I never expected that reaction.

She turned away and walked as fast as she could. I stood still. I looked over at Clegg's farm, then back as Angela went out of sight behind a hawthorn hedge. My last glimpse of her was the sun shining on that lovely red hair. Whatever Angela said, it was down to Clegg. I'd lost her because of him.

*

FOR THE REST of the afternoon I brooded. Angela said we were finished, but we'd hardly started. I'd only met her on the bus ten days ago. Our romance consisted of one visit to the pictures, a few drinks, a walk up the canal bank and the other 'walk' interrupted by Cyril Clegg. Now it was poisoned by him and his wish to get back at me. I lay on my bed for more than an hour after tea wondering how I could hit back at him for spoiling things with Angela, but most of all, for my humiliation by a man I loathed now more than anyone.

I considered firing his barns. I toyed with the idea of filling his tractor tanks with sugar. I wondered about poison pen letters. I even dallied with thoughts of a balaclava helmet, a dark farmyard and a pickaxe handle, but only for a few mad moments. Cyril Clegg had found his way under my skin and I had to deal with him, extract him like a sheep tick, but how? Then it came to me, I knew the answer: Blum. I needed his help and imagination.

Over past months, we'd seen little of each other. He left school after blowing his O-levels. I scraped enough to get into sixth-form. While I tried to work out what to do with my life and started to put more effort in at school, Blum decided to become a long-distance lorry driver. As a first step, he took a job with Daltry's, a firm near Southport who supplied tools, seeds, outdoor clothing and other farm supplies. The firm put him through driving lessons and now he drove one of their vans all over west Lancashire to deliver supplies and take orders. Spending his time out on the road with not much supervision suited his way of life and his character.

I saw him now and then for a pint, or for a few hours' fishing, but he was spending more and more time with Viv. She had been the driving force in their project to finish the renovation of the Chev. Even Uncle Walter developed an interest in the project. The owner had offered to swap it for Blum's four-ten shotgun, once a possession of the signalman. I was there at the negotiations when we met the owner in a pub in Ormskirk. Blum wanted the car, but not enough to give up the gun. For him, the circumstances of acquiring it and the memories attached to it had given the dainty double-barreled gun an iconic status. Instead, he found the cash. Blum always seemed to have money when needed.

That warm March evening I found him outside the Plough Horse. He sat swinging his legs over the edge of the canal bank with an empty pint glass in his hand, a cigarette in the other. He said he was waiting for Viv to finish her shift at the hospital -- where she was a nurse -- before going on to a party at the nurses' hostel. I took his glass and went into the Plough Horse to fetch us two pints of bitter.

When we'd caught up on our news, I brought up meeting Angela and our humiliation by Cyril Clegg. Blum nodded when I told him I wanted to get back at the rat-faced farmer. He was amused by my story, but scathing about Clegg.

'Blummin' sex maniac, that's what he is,' said Blum, 'I heard that from me mam a while ago.'

'You mean before that time he nabbed us?'

Blum laughed, 'When I said I'd blow his brains out? Nah not then, but when I told her he was on my round for work she filled me in on him. I've met him since, loads of times. He knows I put the gun up to him, but if he wants stuff from Daltry's its deal with me or lump it and he could never prove owt any road.'

Blum sipped his pint. 'I call at his place regular. He's a good customer, but guess who's always asking for them nudie calendars we get off the reps at Christmas? He's like a panting dog for them, I'm not kidding.'

'I can imagine, but a few pin-ups don't exactly make him a sex-maniac.'

'I bet it would down the Methodist Church.'

I laughed, 'What?'

'Cyril's a bit of a big-wig there. A lay-preacher, he is. When he's not slavering over his calendars he's down there preaching fire and brimstone, about sin and that. The boss calls him Creeping Jesus.'

'Straight-up?'

Blum blew out smoke, 'With Cyril Clegg, it's not just calendars with big tits and that. It's much worse.'

I was intrigued. Blum said his mam knew a young woman who took on the cleaning at Clegg's farmhouse. He touched her up, really upset her, and her husband put the groping farmer in hospital for a week. The husband wanted him had up in court, but Clegg got a solicitor on the job and the couple settled for a five hundred pound pay-out to keep matters out of the courts.

'All hushed up', said Blum, 'Nobody at his church knew owt about it.'

I whistled. 'Five hundred quid!'

'That's nowt to Cyril Clegg. He's minted.'

'I noticed the new tractor and all the rest of it.'

'I know' said Blum, 'He spends a fortune with us. And he's got stocks and shares all over the show, the boss says.'

Blum took another swig at his pint. 'He wants to expand. I've heard he's trying to get John Sykes' farm off him for a knock-down price.'

'He's the feller who farms next to him?'

'That's him. He's the church-warden at the C of E. Anyway, his missus wants them to sell up and go and live by the sea, or something, but Sykes isn't too keen. He's not too keen on selling to Clegg, either, but the missus is pushing him and nobody else is interested in buying the place.'

'Why won't he sell to Clegg?'

'Well, this is what me mam told me…'

Blum told me that when his mam was younger, a girl had been sexually assaulted, raped, some said, by a man on a public footpath near the two farms one dark night. Sykes had been questioned by the police, but accused Clegg of being the guilty man. Sykes was convinced he was right because he'd seen Clegg hanging about in the area a short time before. He'd also heard tales of Clegg's unhealthy interest in younger women. Nothing had come of the investigation owing to a lack of evidence, but Clegg had slandered Sykes as a liar. Even caused a fuss by writing a letter to the vicar, the parish council, and others, stating Sykes was the guilty man; he even stated he was a rapist. Sykes' late father had been forced to use lawyers to silence Clegg's untruths. Sykes had hated Clegg ever since.

'No wonder he won't sell him the farm.'

'Poor feller's running out of excuses to give his missus, though.'

'Isn't Clegg being a pervert, even a rapist, enough?'

'Mam says Dolly Sykes has never known owt about it.'

I didn't get the chance to ask more as I heard the sound of a powerful engine. Blum drained the rest of his pint in one swig and stood up. A slim figure on a Norton motorbike crossed the swing bridge and did a neat turn on the cinder towpath. Champing gum, Viv smiled and nodded to me, her slim wrist revving the bike. With her razor cut hair and her slight build, kitted out in black leather, she always seemed an odd custodian of such a heavy, powerful machine.

'Thanks for the pint,' Blum said, thrusting his empty glass into my hand.

He threw a leg over the pillion of Viv's bike. She gave me another nod, then sprayed cinders, before she sped back over the wooden bridge in a roar of acceleration. Blum raised a hand in farewell, not looking back.

For the first time ever Blum hadn't come up with an idea. In all the years we'd been mates... Even a couple more pints didn't cheer me up. I felt let down, flattened.

*

THREE DAYS LATER I came home from an after-school cricket practice, conscious that I had a free evening, warm weather and nothing to do. Had Angela still been on the scene, cricket would've been as attractive as a cold shower. I was intrigued to learn from my mum that Blum had called round that afternoon and left me a message to meet up.

I headed straight for the Scottish Soldier as instructed. Blum's work van was parked out front. As I crossed the yard, I saw him through the tiny window of the back parlour. Under the blackened beams, he was standing by the fireplace, his fingers idly tapping the back of his head. I knew what that was about.

The landlord poured two pints of bitter from a tall pewter jug and I carried the dripping glasses through to join Blum. He savoured the fresh pint and took a seat on the settle by the window. I sat beside him.

'Blummin' 'eck, them nurses can sup,' he said, 'I'm only just back in the real world after the other night.'

He shook his head, took another swig at the pint and said, 'Doesn't mean I haven't been thinking about you-know-who, mind...'

I felt a sudden, excited lift and it wasn't from the pint of bitter.

Blum went on, 'What we've got to decide is: what's the most important thing in Cyril Clegg's life? What does that rat-faced bastard want?'

'To touch up young girls, or worse?'

'Nah, nah, that's his hobby, a sick one, mind, but there's summat more.'

'Something to do with the Methodist church?'

'Nope,' Blum said.

'His farm, then?'

'He's already got that.'

'Yeah, but surely...?'

Blum raised a hand to stop me.

'It's expanding the farm. He thinks he's got John Sykes' land in the bag. That's why he's got new stuff -- the tractor, and all the rest of it. If he got

Sykes' place it'd make him the biggest farmer in the parish.'

I cottoned on, 'So you think we can stop him? Screw up his big ideas?'

Blum grinned. 'I'd say it's worth a blummin' try.'

He put his pint aside and pushed his hand into his pocket. He took out a brown envelope and tipped the contents on to the palm of his hand. He held it out to me.

I peered at the black granular pile in his palm.

I looked at him, 'Is that gunpowder?'

Blum chuckled. 'Mixed in with a good dose of bag muck, you know, nitrogen fertiliser, it could be pretty explosive.'

*

A WEEK BEFORE full moon and two days after our meeting at the Soldier, Blum and I sat in his van under the big elder tree outside the C of E church. To one side, Clegg's land rose in a slope. It was gone midnight and we were waiting for Viv to arrive from late shift at the hospital. I queried Viv joining us, but Blum said we needed an extra man -- or woman -- to get the job done.

'What if she chickens out?' I said, 'This isn't exactly legal.'

Blum said that wouldn't happen, 'She's scared of nowt. And I mean nowt.'

Viv's Norton turned into the lane as she throttled back the revs. She killed her lights and the bike coasted to a halt alongside the van. Blum handed out our dark boiler suits and balaclavas and issued the equipment, packed in haversacks, like a commando quartermaster. Blum explained and minutes later we set off in single file up the sloping field in the direction of Clegg's farm.

Blum had planned everything. It was plodding, repetitive work, but far more enjoyable working as a team, than scraping and digging weeds from a quarter acre of overgrown cobbles with a moody red-head. A few minutes before four o'clock the preparations for hitting back at Cyril Clegg were complete. We slunk away from Clegg's place confident we'd not been seen.

As we chucked our gear back in the van, Blum grinned. 'The fuse is laid. Now we just have to wait for the explosion.'

*

IT WAS A long fuse for a delayed action 'bomb' that went off in the second week of June. When Blum knocked me up at quarter to seven as the sun started to burn off the early mist, he was excited. He'd been monitoring Clegg's farm for days on his way to work and this morning his plan had reached fruition. He was impatient to show me its spectacular outcome.

We turned into the lane up to the church and accelerated to the lych-gate. We jumped out of the van and Blum pointed across to Clegg's land. The slope was one of the highest points in our flat landscape. It began at the old sandpits and came down towards the church. I could see the result of our work as clear as a splash headline on the front page of a tabloid newspaper.

In the soft green of thirty acres of half-grown, spring barley were twenty letters. Each letter was twenty-five feet tall and ten feet wide. The letters were composed of thousands of crimson poppies sown from tiny seeds that looked like gunpowder. The five words, which were visible for at least a quarter of a mile, read, JOHN SYKES IS THE RAPIST.

Blum grinned, 'What about that?' he said, in imitation of the man we had targeted, 'Eh, eh?'

I started to laugh. So did my friend. It was just like old times.

*

BLUM RELAYED TO me the repercussions of the words in the barley as his mam picked up the gossip on the parish network:

Full-colour photographs were taken. Locals came to gawp and chatter. John Sykes was furious. Yellowing files were dug out at the family solicitor's office. His wife was outraged -- more so when she found out the full story of Clegg defaming the husband she hadn't then met. Plus one or two accounts of Clegg's unsavoury conduct with young women.

Clegg received a writ for libel and was obliged to settle out of court for a tidy, undisclosed sum. Dolly Sykes spent the settlement money on a seafront flat at Lytham St.Annes for holidays. She agreed with her husband; the farm would not be sold to Clegg if he were the last buyer in the world. The Sykes' wills had new caveats to forbid a sale to Clegg under any future circumstances.

Gossip about Clegg's crimes against young women started to seep out. The Methodist Church had an extraordinary, extraordinary meeting where a confused and puzzled Cyril Clegg protested his innocence before being forced to resign as lay-preacher. And before all that, a fair portion of unripe barley contaminated with thousands of poppies was ploughed in with a new tractor that was soon after up for sale…

I never knew if Angela heard about Clegg's downfall, but nor did I speak to her again. She went away to university and the last I heard a few years later, she married an advertising executive and went to live in Surrey. Now and then I wonder what might have become of us had I let her pay that thirty bob to our local sex offender.

I saw Cyril Clegg many times before his death. He never failed to give me a suspicious stare. I never failed to give him a pleasant smile. In a way, I'm grateful to him. My friendship with Blum had faltered. Thanks to the pervert farmer, it had been renewed. It would last for the rest of his life.

More Blum...

If you enjoyed the Blum stories, look out for the full-length book, *Friends, Lies, Booze and Magpies.*

Winter, 1970...When Blum Gatley is sent to Borstal for theft, his girlfriend, Viv, and his lifelong friend don't understand why he stole from work.--.why he needs money.

But when his friend, a trainee reporter with a potential drink problem, learns of Blum's private and urgent quest, he is sworn to secrecy and promises to help.

He takes time out from his two-timing love life, develops his taste for risk-taking, then joins Blum in a criminal venture that leads him to commit an act of violence when things go wrong. The aftermath culminates on a single day of drunkenness, emotion, attempted murder and tragedy; with repercussions that affect his whole life.--. And keep his lies at full-stretch 30 years into the future.

Though Blum might need cash fast, he is still driven to change for the better the life of another Borstal boy – an unfortunate and innocent lad who has suffered a cruel injustice by the legal system -- and brutality at the hands of a corrupt, sadistic prison officer at a Lancashire Borstal.

Blum and his friends want revenge...

*

BARRY WOODWARD was brought up in Lydiate in the 1950s and 1960s and those times and place inspired these stories. Later, he worked as a reporter, a news editor, a freelance advertising copywriter, a press officer and as a jobbing television scriptwriter on programmes like Channel 4's *Brookside, Hollyoaks* and *The Courtroom*, Yorkshire Television's *Emmerdale* and *Heartbeat*, Thames Talkback's *The Bill* and Granada Television's *In Suspicious Circumstances*, as well as plenty of futile and aborted projects for film and TV. He wrote many articles and had more than 500 scripts produced, some broadcast in more than 50 countries. He once had a *Writer's Guild* nomination, but lost the certificate. He lives near Preston in Lancashire with his wife, Anne, and their cats.

You can reach him at BWLydiateseries@gmail.com

Printed in Great Britain
by Amazon

14676140R00123